Under the scaffold

and what happened to Tom Whittaker

Under the scaffold

and what happened to Tom Whittaker

Faith Cook

EVANGELICAL PRESS

EVANGELICAL PRESS
Faverdale North, Darlington, DL3 0PH, England

e-mail: sales@evangelicalpress.org

Evangelical Press USA
P. O. Box 825, Webster, New York 14580, USA

e-mail: usa.sales@evangelicalpress.org

web: http://www.evangelicalpress.org

First published 2005

British Library Cataloguing in Publication Data available

ISBN-13   978-0-85234-597-9   ISBN 0-85234-597-6

Printed and bound in Great Britain by Creative Print and Design Wales, Ebbw Vale, South Wales.

Contents

		Page
To the reader		7
1.	A crisis for Tom	9
2.	The day the curate called	19
3.	Scotch Will	27
4.	Mad Grimshaw	35
5.	A cry on the moors	43
6.	The night of the storm	51
7.	A prayer God heard	61
8.	A kindness repaid	69
9.	A riot at Roughlee	77
10.	The unforgettable preacher	89
11.	A passing year	95
12.	The old woman on the moors	105
13.	The revenge	113
14.	Kathy	123
15.	Prisoner of hope	133
16.	Forgiven	145
Notes		155

Illustrations

Haworth today	8
View over Haworth Moor	12
William Grimshaw	23
Black Bull, Haworth*	28
Disused quarry on Haworth Moor*	33
Grimshaw's front door*	36
Typical gully on Haworth Moor	46
Snow scene#	59
Charles Wesley	70
John Wesley	80
Site of the Roughlee riot	87
George Whitefield†	93
Entrance to Sowdens	139
Haworth Church in 1756	141
Haworth Church after rebuilding work*	143

*   *Reproduced courtesy of Dr Penny Dickson*
\#   *Reproduced courtesy of Dr Jack Milner*
†   *Reproduced courtesy of Evangelical Library*

To the reader

This book is for all ages: for younger adults as well as older ones, for Tom Whittaker was never a 'teenager' — in fact, the word did not exist in his day. Most children from the age of eight onwards were expected to work long hours either in the home, workshop or farm to help out with the family finances. Girls often married soon after the age of fourteen or fifteen and set up homes of their own.

The narrative is set in Haworth, Yorkshire, where today thousands of people go each year, drawn by the sad, yet fascinating story of the three Brontë sisters and the books they wrote. But not so many know about William Grimshaw (1708-63), who was the curate of the parish seventy years before the Brontës came to the village. During Grimshaw's time amazing things took place in Haworth — much more wonderful than anything that happened in the time of the Brontës. Tom Whittaker, the main character in this book, was born and brought up in Haworth during this period and through his eyes we can discover something of these events.

Although Tom's story is partly fiction, it has been drawn from many true-life incidents. These have been woven together from various sources to form the day-to-day experiences of one boy and his family. On the other hand, everything that is written about William Grimshaw himself, and also of John and Charles Wesley and George Whitefield, is completely factual. All the important things they say are taken from their recorded words or writings.

So now find out what happened to Tom 'under the scaffold'.

Faith Cook

Haworth today

I.
A crisis for Tom

Tom Whittaker scrambled up the rough moorland path. At times he slid back helplessly as loose stones and shale suddenly shifted beneath his feet. Regaining his balance, and spurred onwards by an inner urgency to leave his home, his village and his sorrows far behind him, Tom clambered on. At last he reached a hidden dell, a spot which he and his sister Alice had only recently discovered. Here he could sit unseen by anyone. Sheltered by the long grasses that swayed gently in the wind and by the great grey boulders that stood like silent sentinels around him, Tom pressed his face into his hands and began to cry quietly. But eight-year-olds don't cry, he told himself, as he brushed away the tears fiercely with the back of his hand.

Tom and Alice Whittaker had been inseparable. Those who did not know the family often mistook them for twins for both were fair-haired with the same clear blue eyes and much the same in height. But there the likeness ended. Tom was a talkative, mischievous eight-year-old with an endless store of bright ideas, many of which led him into trouble. Alice was seven; a trustful, attractive child, who adored her older brother. Despite his unpredictable and impetuous nature, her loyalty to him was unwavering, particularly when some fresh escapade called down the wrath of their father, Jack Whittaker, on her brother's head. When Tom had decided to have a ride on the back of one of the sows that his father reared, not surprisingly, the animal had panicked. Boy and pig hurtled round and round the farmyard, Tom holding on desperately to the sow's ears to avoid being thrown to the ground. At last he managed to roll off safely. It was Alice who pleaded his cause when Tom faced a just penalty for his misdeed. The unfortunate pig had been so frightened that she gave premature birth to her litter of young, most of whom had died — an event that had serious implications for a family as poor as the Whittaker family.

Jack and Mary Whittaker farmed a smallholding known as Old Acre Farm on the outskirts of Haworth, a small Yorkshire village high up in the Pennines. They found it hard, very hard, to support their family on the income that Jack could gain from the sale of farm produce and young pigs. Mary also had to help, working long hours as she spun the wool from the fleeces of their small flock of long-haired sheep. The previous winter had been long and bitter, but with the sudden rise in temperatures during late spring the snows had melted and flood waters had cascaded down the moor bringing devastation to many homes. Worse than this, however, was the onset of yet another epidemic of typhus fever that appeared to accompany the change in weather. Sweeping through the village, the virulent infection was taking its toll of young lives and leaving many desolate families behind.

Every mother in Haworth watched her children anxiously, and it was with sinking heart that Mary Whittaker noticed Alice's flushed cheeks, followed by a soaring temperature. Before long the unmistakable symptoms of typhus fever became evident. The Whittakers were so poor they could not even afford to purchase the most basic medicines to relieve Alice's fever and her aching head. The thought of summoning the local apothecary, as the village doctor was called, was certainly beyond their slender means.

Tom loved Alice and was clearly distressed at his sister's illness. Perhaps she was going to die. He did not know. He had heard of other children in the village who had died in the epidemic. What would happen if she were taken from him? Tom was often in trouble but Alice had always stood up for him and Jack Whittaker could not resist his small daughter when she turned her big, innocent-looking blue eyes on him. She had saved her older brother from many a sharp sting from the cane Jack kept on the shelf above the kitchen fire.

When Alice was no better after three days, Tom could bear it no longer. Rushing from the cottage that morning he had climbed high up the moor to the hidden nook where he and Alice had played a few days earlier. At least no one would find him up there and perhaps, he thought hopefully, when he went back to the farm everything would be all right after all. At that moment a skylark sprang unexpectedly from the long grasses not far from where Tom was sitting. Perhaps the boy was too near the bird's nest. A curious child, he began to search around to see if he could find a nest with its clutch of speckled brown eggs. But if the skylark had a nest nearby, it was too well hidden for Tom to discover, so he began to watch the bird instead as it mounted higher and higher into the sky above him. Up and up it soared until it was a mere speck in the distant blue. Then he caught the sweet sound of its singing floating downwards to where he sat. What was beyond that high dome of sky? he wondered. Was heaven there somewhere? And if Alice died, would her soul be taken up there, far, far away from him? Tom had no answers to his questions.

A new curate had just come to Haworth. His name was William Grimshaw, a big burly sort of man, not at all Tom's idea of a

View over Haworth Moor

curate, and he had heard him say something that the boy could not easily forget. 'Today is your living day. Tomorrow may be your dying day.' How true that was, and all the people of Haworth knew it only too well. But it was not something Tom wanted to hear and it did nothing more than add to his distress as he thought of Alice crying out in pain in her small hot bedroom. As Tom peered far down beneath him, he could just see the parish church — the church that had the grand name of St Michael's and All Angels. And even at that very moment he could see small figures moving around the churchyard. Perhaps they were burying yet another child, snatched away at the beginning of life by that dreadful typhus epidemic. Tom began to cry again.

'What ails thee, little 'un?' said a rough kindly voice just behind him. Tom started and looked up. He had not heard anyone approaching. Farmer Greenwood, the shepherd from a neighbouring farm further up the moor than Old Acre, had seen the small figure perched high up on the moor side and had come to see who it could be. 'Eh, nowt,' said Tom hurriedly. But then he blurted out, 'My sister's so ill, and I dinna know what to do.'

The weather-beaten face of the farmer clouded over. 'I don't know but there's much yer can do,' he admitted slowly at last. 'But you go home and be a good boy' — Tom had gained quite a reputation for his mischievous pranks — 'and maybe she'll be right ere long.' Tom smiled faintly. The comfort of another human voice cheered him, even if his friend knew no solutions. Slowly Tom rose and the two together — an old man and a child — made their way cautiously down the rough track.

It was a late spring day in 1743. All the world seemed to be laughing as new life burst from bush and tree alike. The air was filled with bird song and spring flowers brought a splash of colour against the drab grey stones of Tom's cottage home. But there was little laughter inside the home that day. Parting from his shepherd friend, Tom slipped quietly in at the back door. No one seemed to have missed him. Margaret, his eleven-year-old sister, a conscientious if rather bossy girl, was in the kitchen trying to make a meal for the family. Molly, who was still only thirteen months old, sat cheerfully enough at her older sister's feet, carefully examining a chipped enamel cup from which she had been drinking. George was nowhere to be seen. Perhaps the four-year-old was with his father, watching him swill out the pigsty in the field behind the house.

'How's Alice?' Tom asked apprehensively.

'She's bin calling for yer,' Margaret replied, 'you'd best go an' see her.' With a heavy heart Tom mounted the stairs and entered the room where Alice was lying. Beside her bed sat his mother, anxiously trying to cool the child's burning skin with damp cloths, despair written in every line of her face. When Alice saw Tom she stretched out both arms to him. 'I'll do that for yer now, Ma,' said Tom, as he approached the bed: a strange task for an eight-year-old. But Tom remembered the old shepherd's words. Perhaps if he did all he could to be helpful and to stay out of mischief his sister would recover, he told himself.

The low heavy beams of the attic bedroom which Tom shared with Alice sloped almost to the floor. The only light came from two narrow windows set in the roof. Badly fitted, they would rattle and shake in the gale-force winds of winter that often howled around the cottage. They were patched up with paper in an attempt to prevent the rain from seeping in through the cracks. The uneven wooden floorboards sloped precariously in line with the gradient of the hillside into which the cottage had been built. In summer the room became oppressively hot and even today the atmosphere was heavy with the pungent smell that accompanies typhus fever. Alice was flushed, her usually bright eyes dull and heavy, and the characteristic rash was beginning to make its appearance on her face and arms. But she was grateful for Tom's attention and pleased to have him nearby.

Tom glanced around the small room. It was sparsely furnished with little else apart from the children's beds, the three-legged stool on which he was sitting, and an old oak chest in one corner where their clothes were stored. Although Jack Whittaker toiled for long hours on his small farmstead to keep his family clothed and fed, he found the draw of the *Black Bull Inn*, a tavern that stood close by the church itself, an irresistible one. Each evening he could be found squandering his hard-earned coppers, drinking ale with the men of the village.

Old Acre Farm was built on land belonging to the church and so the monthly rent which Jack Whittaker had to pay formed part of the curate's salary. This arrangement meant that each month the curate would be sure to knock on the Whittakers' front door to collect the rent due to him. When Isaac Smith, the previous incumbent of the parish, had been curate the calls had been formal enough; since the arrival of the new curate no visit from William Grimshaw would pass without him urging the family to be more regular in their attendance at St Michael's. 'If you will not come to church to hear me, you shall hear me at home,' he had said on his last visit, and concluded with a threat that had startled Jack and Mary Whittaker, uttered in a broad Yorkshire dialect, 'An' if tha perish tha will perish w' t' sound o' t' gospel i' yer lugs!'[1] It had frightened Tom as well, and made him feel angry inside. How could that curate say a thing like that to people who could not even afford to buy clothes that were good enough to attend church?

Tom was glad when Margaret called to tell him that dinner was ready. His climb up to the moor had sharpened his appetite. The smell of onions boiled in milk wafted through the house and, together with a chunk of rye bread, was a typical meal for the Whittaker family. Occasionally a piece of bacon might supplement their diet, but this was rare for all the pork produced by the pigs that Jack Whittaker reared in the shed at the back of the house had to be sold for the best price that it could command. The family was not in the habit of giving thanks to God before a meal and as he chewed hungrily on his bread, Tom smiled wryly to himself. Someone had told him that recently the new curate had been heard saying that those who ate without giving thanks were worse than the pigs — and as his father reared pigs Tom remembered the words: 'Some of you,' he had said pointedly, 'are worse than the very swine; for the pigs will *grunt* over their victuals, but you say nothing.'

However, Tom was not really in the mood for smiling today. That curate does not understand what it is like to go hungry, he thought bitterly, nor does he know what it is like to be unable to buy medicines when someone is sick. If he were in our house for a few days he might think differently. Even at that moment he could hear Alice crying out for her mother. Wiping his mouth, Tom left the table to find his father and George to tell them that their meal was ready. Sure enough his father was in the shed with his younger son. As Tom entered, Jack's eyes lit up for he and Tom had always been close. Even though Tom had often felt the force of his father's brawny arm across his backside, or experienced the stinging impact of a cuff on the ear as a punishment for some misdemeanour, there was a basic and deep understanding between them.

One of Tom's daily tasks was to fetch water for the family from the Head Well pump at the top of the village, a supply that met the needs of almost half of the Haworth households. Collecting his buckets from behind the shed, the boy set off. At this time of the year the springs that fed the well ran freely, for the melting snows added to the volume of water; but at the height of summer Tom would often set off before dawn to wait his turn to fill his buckets from the trickling supply. Although he did not know it, the underground spring which supplied the Head Well pump ran so close to the village burying ground that surrounded the church that the water he carried home was often contaminated. In fact during the hot weather it could become so putrid that even the cattle, as they were driven to the nearby troughs to drink, had been known to turn away without satisfying their thirst. Undoubtedly this circumstance added to the many illnesses that the Whittaker family suffered, illnesses that carried away nearly half the children of Haworth to an early grave before they had reached the age of seven.[2]

With his buckets full, Tom stepped carefully over the open gutters that ran down Main Street. With no sewage system in the village, household waste, rubbish, butcher's offal and sewage all ran freely down the steep incline. Usually the offensive stream emptied itself into the River Worth that ran along the valley, but some was collected in cesspits in the open fields — once again forming a ready breeding ground for the many germs that carried the diseases that troubled and terrified the people.

Back along West Lane Tom trudged, sometimes slopping water over the sides of his buckets, sometimes stopping to rest for a few moments, and all the time wondering what situation would greet him when he arrived back. Then Tom took a short cut across the fields to reach his home but carefully avoided passing too close to Sowdens, the newly-built farmstead where the curate, William Grimshaw, lived with his wife and children. Sowdens had its own spring of fresh running water, and with a pang of jealousy Tom thought about the curate's son John, a boy of almost his own age. 'He has never had to carry water like this,' he thought. Jane Grimshaw, the curate's younger child, was the same age as Alice, but Tom had never seen her.

At last he arrived at his own front door. Little had changed since he left more than a hour earlier. His sister Margaret had been busy pulling out the burrs and other unwanted bits from the fleeces of their newly-shorn sheep that grazed on the grassy slopes above their home. Then she would have to comb the wool in readiness for her mother to spin. As Alice had fallen into an uneasy sleep, Mary Whittaker had returned to her spinning wheel. Due to her child's illness, she had become sadly behind in her work. Jack was anxious to take the spun skeins of wool to Bradford on Sunday for sale at the market and little time now remained. Thankfully Tom rested his aching arms for a short while and then wandered off in search of his friends.

2.
The day the curate called

Throughout the next few days Tom did all he could to be helpful. He ran errands, and carried fuel to stoke up the old iron stove in the kitchen. He even hoed the weeds that were growing on the vegetable patch where Jack cultivated the food needed for his family. Tom resisted the temptation to trip up his younger brother whenever he found George annoying; he clenched his fists tightly when he felt like slapping him in the face for some of his cheeky remarks. He did his best to be attentive to Alice's needs and all the time the words of old Farmer Greenwood rang in his ears: 'Go home and be a good boy and maybe she'll be right ere long.' Perhaps the God that the curate preached about would see how hard he was trying and would make Alice better, he thought desperately. Mary looked anxiously at her tousled-headed son. She knew how strongly he felt about everything: about the farm, about the moors, about how hard his father had to work, but most of all about his sister Alice. She feared that Tom would take it very badly if Alice died.

Even Tom could see that Alice was not improving. She lay so still. She did not cry so much now. When her mother tried gently to coax her to eat a little bread softened in milk, she just shook her head and turned her face to the wall. Then one morning Alice did not wake up at all. Tom crossed over to her bed and shook her urgently to try to rouse her. 'Alice, Alice, wake up,' he whispered. Although Alice was breathing lightly, she did not respond. That morning Tom rushed out of the house without waiting for any breakfast.

Up and up he climbed, farther than he had ever ventured before on to the moor. At last he found a spot where a small stream chuckled and gurgled between the boulders as it rushed on its way down the hillside. Here he sat: for how long, he never knew. He was not crying now, just staring in front of him, seeing nothing. He had tried so hard to be good and it had not worked. Alice was going to die after all. The small knot of bitterness tightened in his chest. Now he would be bad — as bad as he wanted to be, he determined. What was the purpose of trying to be good? The sky was the same blue as it had ever been; the birds sang as loudly as ever, the flowers still brightened the moors; but all seemed to have changed in Tom's world.

At last as a cool wind sprang up and hunger pangs began to gnaw at his stomach, Tom stood up, stretched his legs and set his face towards his home. It must have been early afternoon by the time the village came in sight. He hesitated as he reached his own front door. What would he find when he entered? But one glance at his mother, her eyes red, her face swollen with crying, told him all he needed to know. Grabbing a chunk of bread from the kitchen table, Tom hurried around to the shed, picked up his buckets and set off to the Head Well pump to collect the water.

The funeral took place two days later. It was a quiet affair, with very few mourners to sympathize with the family over the loss of Alice. Most of the villagers had already fled from Haworth to escape the epidemic. Only those with no relatives in nearby places, or with commitments which they could not leave, remained. But Mary was comforted to see her close friend

The day the curate called

Jeanie Hartley there, together with her older daughter Kathy. Jeanie and Mary had been childhood friends and now, with her husband Robert, Jeanie farmed a smallholding not far from Old Acre known as Meadow Head Farm. Alice and Kathy had been the same age and the two children had often played together when Tom was helping his father on the farm.

Old Farmer Greenwood also came to the funeral, sitting by himself at the back of the church. As he glanced at Tom's white face, the tears flowed down his old cheeks. He thought of the boy's unspoken distress, remembering that day so short a time ago when he had discovered the child crying alone on the moors. He remembered too what he had said to Tom that day, and wondered if the boy had taken his words to heart.

Tom, for his part, sat with clenched fists. At one point he squeezed his eyes tightly shut to stop any tears creeping out, tears that would betray how upset he was. He listened numbly to the sermon. He could not understand much of what the curate was saying, but one or two strange remarks penetrated his troubled thoughts: 'Time ere long will be to you time no longer…' Certainly that was true for his poor little sister, so young, so cheerful and easy-going. 'Your time is short and your work is great. You have a Christ to believe in, a God to honour…' and then something about 'a soul to save, a hell to escape and a heaven to gain…' It was all too difficult for Tom and he shut himself off from the rest of the sermon. Mechanically he followed his parents and Margaret into the windswept churchyard where a shallow grave had been dug for the coffin that carried away all that remained of his favourite sister Alice.

Three days had passed since the funeral — days when the family went about its usual tasks with few words spoken. Molly alone remained her lively self, and it brought a faint smile to Mary Whittaker's face when her baby took her first few uncertain steps, and then promptly collapsed heavily on the floor beaming with delight over her latest achievement. Jack Whittaker, an emotional and tender-hearted man, spent longer at the *Black Bull Inn* than usual, sometimes not returning until late at night, and then far from sober. Tom scowled and kicked angrily at the stones in the farmyard. Even the pigs seemed wary of him and squealed and grunted as he approached.

It was Tom who first heard the heavy footsteps approaching Old Acre Farm. He knew instinctively that it was William Grimshaw, the curate — come to collect the rent, no doubt, thought Tom resentfully. Grimshaw bent his head to avoid hitting it on the low lintel, and entered the room. Mary had been working at the spinning wheel; her white face was the only hint of her inner pain. Margaret was combing the long threads in readiness for her mother to spin. Tom disappeared from the room, first of all to call his father, but then to escape off by himself. He had no wish to see the curate at that moment. But something about the curate's face made him hesitate and change his mind. There was a look of concern and tenderness in his eyes that Tom had never noticed before. No, he had not come to collect the rent. He had come to comfort the family over the loss of Alice, and to encourage them yet again to attend the church more regularly.

As Tom sat on a stool in the corner, he fixed his eyes steadily on Mr Grimshaw. In an irrational way he felt that the curate was partly to blame for his sister's death. If God was so powerful, so strong as the curate had told them that he was, surely Grimshaw could have prayed to him for Alice and she would have recovered. Almost before he could control himself he blurted out, 'Tha's niver lost someun tha loves, has tha?' With a movement astonishingly swift for a big man, Grimshaw swirled round and fixed his eyes on the child in the corner of the room.

'Tom, Tom,' he said gently, 'I lost someone I loved more than anyone else in the world. When the mother of my two children died, I didna want to live any longer. Sarah was young and pretty. Her laughter made our home a happy place, but when John was three and Jane only two, I buried my Sarah down Luddenden, in the parish church.' Tom was silent now.

This time Jack Whittaker spoke. 'And did the God you tell us about help you in the darkness?' was his searching yet sincere question.

'Yes,' answered Grimshaw steadily, 'but it didn't seem so at first. I even wrote out instructions for my own funeral, for I wished for nothing except to follow Sarah to the grave. Wicked thoughts crowded into my mind. I often felt ready to accuse God

William Grimshaw

23

of dealing harshly with someone who was trying to please him.' Every eye in the room was now fixed earnestly on the speaker. He seemed to Tom to be echoing the boy's own inmost thoughts. 'I had tried so hard to please God by my good works,' Grimshaw continued. 'I had even made a list of all the good deeds and all the bad deeds I had done in a single day and hoped that the good deeds would cancel out the bad ones in God's sight.'

'What happened next?' asked Tom, now following every word the curate spoke. 'Well, I went on like that for almost two years, until one day just over two years ago now, a strange thing happened. I went into a friend's house, to a room quite like this one. On the table lay a book — I like books, you see, so I went to pick it up. Just at that moment there was a very odd flash of light. I didna know where it came from. I looked at the fire, but it was burning low. So I turned back and picked up the book from the table, and though you might find it hard to believe, I felt another uncommon beam of heat and light flashing in my face. Perhaps it was being reflected from the pewter dishes that were standing on the shelf opposite the fire, I thought, now really puzzled. Then I opened the book and began to glance at the first page. I had only read a few lines when suddenly a third flash of heat struck me. Then I understood. God was telling me that I had to read that book, and that he had something to say to me in it.'[1]

'And did he?' asked Tom.

'Do you really believe things like that happen?' persisted Jack Whittaker in a voice that scarcely hid his incredulity.

'Aye,' Grimshaw continued, 'because in that book I learnt at last that none of my good deeds were good enough for God. Only the goodness of Jesus could make me really good. When I understood this, I was at last willing to give up every little bit of my own goodness that I fancied I had and to take Christ to be everything to me. O what light and comfort I then had deep in my soul! What a taste of the forgiving love of God!'

The curate's ugly though strangely attractive face beamed with an inward joy as he recollected that moment. By this time Tom had lost the drift of the conversation, but his mother had her eyes fixed on the curate. Clearly he cared for the Whittaker family and felt deeply for them in their loss. It seemed that he wanted them to share the comfort that he had known.

'But I can't understand the Bible,' confessed Mary timidly. 'Did you find you could understand it after that?'

With a smile Grimshaw answered enthusiastically, 'Why yes, if God had drawn up his Bible into heaven and sent me down another, it could not have been newer to me.'

At that moment Molly woke from her sleep and began to cry. As Mary rose to lift the baby, Grimshaw turned to pick up his hat. But before he left he told the family that he had recently started services in Sowdens on a Sunday night for parishioners who felt too embarrassed about their poor clothes to attend the parish church regularly. He would be glad indeed to see them there. With those words he stripped away the last excuse that Mary Whittaker had raised in her mind against attending many of the services of the church. She now decided that she and her elder daughter Margaret would walk across to Sowdens on Sunday evenings. She knew she could not persuade Jack to come, but in due course Tom might join them too.

But Tom was nowhere to be seen. He did not understand much of what the curate had been saying, and was beginning to cry again as he thought of poor Alice, buried under that cold ground on a beautiful spring day. He could not bear to let Mr Grimshaw see him cry. Although some of the things that the curate had told them were so similar to his own thoughts and feelings, he was far from ready to accept what he had heard. So instead of waiting until the curate had disappeared up the lane, Tom was already making his way up the moor to visit Farmer Greenwood — perhaps he at least would be able to understand how he felt.

He found his old friend sharpening up his shearing tools on the worn old grindstone, for it was already past time to start the shearing. Some of the early lambs were nearly as big as their mothers. The shaggy long-haired coats of his sheep were looking heavy and ragged and he depended on the sale of his wool for his meagre income. Farmer Greenwood lived alone. His wife had died many years ago, and he had few visitors to his isolated farmstead.

'Right sorry, I am about your Alice,' said Farmer Greenwood kindly as Tom entered his small room. Tom did not reply, and wisely the old man did not ply him with questions. At last Tom said, 'I did try to be good, Mr Greenwood, I did really, but it didn't work and Alice still died. Now I'm going to be bad.'

'Tha maun [mustn't] speak like that,' replied his friend, 'it aint right.'

'The curate said he tried to be good for two years,' retorted Tom defensively, 'and if it didna work for him, why do yer think it will for me?' Farmer Greenwood did not reply. Instead he fetched the boy a drink of fresh goat's milk, and let him sit in the kitchen until he was ready to return home.

3.
Scotch Will

'Have yer bin cryin', Tom?' teased George, as he noticed his brother's red tear-blotched face. These were not happy days for Tom Whittaker. His father had just punished him yet again for the way he had spoken to his mother when she asked him to fetch some more wood for the fire. Why should he be the one to do all the unpleasant jobs? Tom had demanded angrily. George, who was now five, was always quick to torment his older brother whenever he spotted an opportunity. The next moment it was George who was crying as he lay flat on his face on the hard flagstones of the kitchen floor. Once more, with a swift movement of one foot, Tom had sent his brother crashing to the ground — only this time George had knocked his head on the side of the kitchen table as he fell. A large swelling was making its appearance on his forehead.

Realizing he was in yet further trouble, Tom quickly ran to the cowshed. There in the dark, he leaned his head against the family cow's warm flank, waiting anxiously as he heard his father calling his name. Then Jack decided to ignore his son's erratic behaviour for the moment and return to his tasks. There in the gloom of the cowshed Tom began to think of all the times he had been in trouble since Alice had died. He missed his sister badly. She alone had listened seriously to all his endless chatter and secret plans. Now there was no one to speak up for him, no one to comfort him when he had been caned for some wrongdoing. To Tom's mind he was being unfairly singled out and blamed for everything that went wrong in the family. In fact, he was largely the cause of most of the trouble. Margaret ignored him, and acted in a very superior way — and after all, she was three years his senior. George could do no wrong in his mother's eyes. All the affection she had poured on Alice seemed to have been transferred to George. But in his heart Tom knew that he himself was at fault. He had deliberately chosen to behave as badly as he wished. Certainly it had made him no happier.

The Whittaker family had known hard times since Alice's death. The cost of the funeral had left them with little money to spare, and Tom had not made things any easier by his rude, uncontrolled behaviour. But instead of saving what little he could, Jack Whittaker had allowed his grief at the loss of

Black Bull, *Haworth*

his daughter to make him an even more regular customer at the *Black Bull,* each night exchanging his hard-earned money, so urgently needed by his family, for the liquor that was slowly destroying him.

With winter approaching Jack realized he would not be able to keep his four children warm and adequately fed during the bitter weather that lay ahead. Tom needed new shoes — already his toes were protruding through the worn leather — and his coat was threadbare. George could wear Tom's cast-offs, but Tom was now nine years of age and growing fast. His coat sleeves came halfway up his arms, and even the patches which Margaret had sewn on to his trousers could no longer hide the holes. Another matter was worrying Jack Whittaker: the monthly rent was almost due. Any day now William Grimshaw would be back at his door to collect his dues.

Two days later the same heavy tread was heard approaching Old Acre Farm. At first Jack decided to pretend he was out — but that would only postpone the moment when he would have to confess to the curate that he did not have the money to pay the rent. Opening the heavy oak door, he looked into Grimshaw's cheery honest face. 'I'm right sorry, Parson,' he began abjectly, 'but I aint got the money this month. Y'see, since our Alice died things have been that tough…' his voice trailed off. The look on the curate's face told him that he knew well enough why Jack Whittaker could not pay. 'But I need the money myself,' insisted the curate whose generosity to those in want often led him into debt himself. 'I fear you will have to pay.'

At that moment Mary appeared at the door. In her arms she was carrying Molly, and the small face of five-year-old George peered out from behind his mother's skirt. Grimshaw looked at the little family. 'I'll be back,' he said simply. Perhaps the curate was going to allow them a further few days to find the money, thought Jack. The next day Tom was in the kitchen when he heard the sound of a horse's hooves approaching the house. Surprised, he went to the front door. The curate was coming, this time leading his white mountain pony. Across the animal's back were slung two large bags of flour. 'Thought these might be useful to you,' he said. 'Here, Tom, help me carry them in for your mother.' Astonished at such kindness shown at a time of need, Tom began to learn a new respect for the curate.

William Grimshaw had something else to tell the family. He planned to reopen the village school: it had enough chairs, tables and books for up to forty boys to be taught basic reading and writing. With a twinkle in his eye, he turned to Tom. 'Thought you might like to come along when we open,' he suggested. 'My boy, John, will be there. I'm sure you will be good friends.' Tom liked John, who was almost the same age as he was, and who was already gaining a reputation among the village boys for daring and mischief. But whether he wanted to attend the school or not was another question. A voice behind him suddenly replied, 'Yes, Tom would like to come, thank you, Parson.' When Jack Whittaker made up his mind, Tom certainly had no options.

By the time the curate had ridden off down the lane, it was mid-afternoon. Tom had not yet collected the water. Grabbing the buckets he set off at quick pace towards the village. He arrived to discover people swarming everywhere. Clearly something unusual was afoot. One name was to be heard on every side. 'Scotch Will has come…' 'Have you heard about Scotch Will?' 'Scotch Will is going to preach outside the *Black Bull*.' Filling his buckets, Tom lingered around to see if he could catch a glimpse of this 'Scotch Will'.

Suddenly a hush descended. Leaving his buckets, Tom wormed his way through to the front of the crowd. There, standing on some steps not far from the tavern was the largest man Tom had ever seen. His rough clothes, shoulder-length hair and bearded face gave him a terrifying appearance. Apparently, so Tom learnt, Scotch Will was a travelling pedlar who hawked his wares from village to village: handkerchiefs, stockings, shoes and many other items. When he had finished selling all that he had brought with him, Scotch Will turned preacher. At that moment a loud voice with a heavy Scottish accent broke the silence. William Darney, for that was his real name, was beginning to preach. He started by denouncing the sins which he knew were freely committed among the people: lying, cheating, cruelty, thieving — the list seemed endless. For all these things men and women would come under the judgement of God, the preacher thundered. Tom shivered. He did not wish to hear any more for he knew only too well that he was guilty of some of those things and more besides, which the preacher did not name. Deftly he threaded his way back through the crowd of packed listeners, for he was a wiry youngster. Collecting his buckets, he made his way homeward.

'I wonder what Mr Grimshaw thinks of Scotch Will,' he thought to himself as he went along. His father, who picked up the local gossip on his nightly trips to the *Black Bull* tavern, knew more than Tom did. No, Mr Grimshaw had not been at all happy about Scotch Will coming to Haworth. He feared that he might be teaching his people to believe the wrong things. But apparently he had attended a private meeting where William Darney was preaching, and had not been able to find any fault with what he was saying.

The next day dawned bright and clear. An early frost tinged the air and the cobwebs were shining silver in the bushes and hedges. It would be a grand day to be up on the moor with his friends, thought Tom. The lads of the village had found a level spot where they enjoyed a rough game of football. Their simple ball, made of animal skin stuffed with horsehair, was far past its best and splitting at the sides, but the boys did not mind.

'Tom,' called his father urgently, just as his son was about to disappear. 'I've got to go to Bradford today to collect some money owing to me. We need it, Tom, and I want you to clean out the pigsties for me while I'm out.' Tom's face fell. 'But Pa…' he began. It was no use. Jack Whittaker was already out of the house. Tom hated cleaning out the pigs. The stench made him feel sick, and in addition, he had never done it on his own before. It would take several hours and then it would be too late to join the other lads for a game.

With a bad spirit Tom set about his unwelcome task, scowling to himself. He would get it done as quickly as possible, even if it meant spending less time on it than he knew he should. He must first sweep out the muck, then swill down the troughs, fetch fresh water for the animals, and put down clean straw on the rough mud floor. Although he would not admit it, he was actually a little nervous of the pigs. His ride on the back of one had not helped and then one large sow had tried to attack him when he had approached too close to her piglets.

At last the chore was almost complete. Just at that moment Tom heard a voice calling him. 'Tom, Tom, where are yer? We're all waiting for yer, Tom,' shouted his friend James.

'Comin',' yelled Tom, and rushed out of the pig shed. In his hurry he failed to secure the lock on the door, and was soon off with the other village lads. Cheerful and hungry, Tom returned home several hours later only to find his mother standing on the doorstep, dismay written all over her face. 'Yer scoundrel, Tom, just look what yer've done!' she exclaimed, pointing to the pig shed. The door was standing wide open. All six of the pigs had escaped and were happily grunting and guzzling in the family allotment. Young winter cabbages which Jack had so carefully sown had been torn from the ground and had either been eaten or were lying on their sides, roots in the air, leaves battered and torn. The onions were not to the pigs' taste, but they had been uprooted all the same. The family's supply of winter vegetables lay devastated before their eyes. There was nothing they could do about the situation until Jack arrived home. 'I dunno what yer pa's goin' t' do wi' yer this time,' said Tom's mother heavily, 'but one thing's for sure. There's no dinner for tha today, my boy.'

With a heart like lead and an empty stomach, Tom retraced his footsteps back to the moor. Angry, ashamed and fearful of the consequences of his carelessness, his mind was in a turmoil. He was old enough to realize that the damage the pigs had caused was serious, particularly in view of the family's lack of money to buy vegetables in the market. Yet at only nine years of age, Tom was still young enough to feel that the loss of his dinner and the beating that would surely follow that night was unjust — even cruel. He hardly cared where he was going, and had no eyes for the beauty of the moor, clothed in purple heather as far as the eye could see. At last he came to a disused quarry and there sat sulking on an upturned stone, muttering rebelliously to himself.

Disused quarry on Haworth Moor

Under the scaffold

He had not been there long before he thought he could hear the sound of voices carried faintly on the wind. He stood up and listened. Yes. It was voices and they were coming from another disused quarry higher up the moor.

But who could it be? Taking a few steps towards the sounds, he stopped to listen again. Now he could hear the words clearly. 'Hark!' said one man. 'I think I hear someone coming.' 'Nay,' replied the other in a voice that sounded strangely familiar — a voice Tom was sure he had heard before somewhere. ''Tis only the sound o' dogs barking in the village.' As Tom moved a little closer the first man spoke again. 'None must ever know that I have spoke w' ye.' Suddenly Tom recognized that second voice only too well. It was none other than that of the curate, William Grimshaw. And the broad Scottish accent of the other must certainly be the voice of Scotch Will. Whatever could they be doing talking in a secret place among the old quarries? And why must no one know? Tom could not tell, but he had enough sense to take to his heels; stumbling and slipping he ran down the moor until he arrived breathless at his own front door.

All thoughts of the strange meeting on the moors between Scotch Will and William Grimshaw were soon far from Tom's mind as he caught sight of his father's face, looking like a thunder cloud. 'Before yer feel the power of my arm, m'lad, yer goin' to help me get them swine back to the sty, and if yer starves this winter yer know who's t' blame,' were his words of greeting. A sorry boy crept into his bed that night, his backside aching, his eyes smarting with unshed tears. He looked across to Alice's empty bed. 'If only you were back,' he whispered. Perhaps these things would not have happened if she had been there. With no one to see him in the darkness he began to sob freely, self-pity and regret mingling his tears.

4.
Mad Grimshaw

A young boy stood timidly outside the forbidding front door
of Sowdens Parsonage. To Tom's nervous gaze the door
resembled the gate of a prison. Built up of two thick layers of
timber, clamped together by more iron bolts than Tom could
count, its massive iron hinges and locks seemed designed to
keep out an army of burglars.

Tom's first knock was so gentle that no one inside could have
heard. How long he waited for someone to come, he did not
know. Then with new boldness born of desperation he lifted both
fists and banged on the door so fiercely that his hands stung with
pain from the bolts.

Slowly the huge door creaked open and to Tom's surprise the
face of a young girl peered out. Dark-haired and petite, Jane
Grimshaw gazed at the poorly-dressed lad who stood outside.
For a swift moment her kindly demeanour reminded Tom of
Alice. Jane was a year younger than Tom, and he remembered
that the curate had said that she was only two when her mother
had died. She had a stepmother now whom Tom had never
seen. 'Who art tha'?' Jane enquired shyly.

'I'm Tom from down Old Acre, an' I've brought your Papa his
money for the rent,' said Tom in a rush.

Picture of Grimshaw's front door

'Who is it, Jane?' called a woman's voice from within. Elizabeth Grimshaw came to the door and looked at the fair-haired boy on the doorstep. 'Come inside, Tom,' she said kindly. Mr Grimshaw isn't here. He's always out preachin' somewhere, and when he aint preachin' he's up there in that attic aprayin'.' Her voice carried a slight note of bitterness which surprised Tom. But he stepped inside and found himself in the kitchen, a large pleasant room with its thick limestone walls, recently whitewashed. A fire glowed in the great fireplace — a fireplace which looked about eight feet wide — for the weather was already turning cold. But what attracted Tom's attention more than anything else was Mr Grimshaw's table. Never had the boy seen a table like it. Supported by six heavily carved curved legs, its oak top seemed to fill the room. Like the front door itself, it appeared to have been built to last until the end of the world.

Quickly placing the money on the table, Tom started for the door. 'Just a moment, Tom,' said Jane's stepmother, 'take yon oatcakes with yer. Sure I am yer mother will be glad o' 'em.' Elizabeth Grimshaw might not be in sympathy with her husband's work, but she was a warm-hearted motherly woman and like everyone else had been sorry to hear that her neighbour's child had died in the typhus epidemic the previous spring. She placed a bag of oatcakes, still warm from the oven, into Tom's hand as he hurried out of the door.

Stuffing an oatcake into his mouth as he crossed the fields to his home, Tom found himself wondering about Jane Grimshaw. Perhaps one day he might get to know her and they could be friends. She might even take Alice's place in his affection. But for now the barrier between the curate's daughter and the poor boy from Old Acre Farm meant that they would rarely meet. No sooner had he reached home than Mary Whittaker reminded Tom that he had not yet fetched the water. 'Can yer take George with yer?' she asked. 'He's bin botherin' me that much all day.'

Anxious to make up for his carelessness in letting the pigs out the previous day, Tom took his younger brother's hand and together they went to collect the buckets. On reaching Head Well pump the boys were astonished to find an even greater number gathered than earlier that week. It seemed that some sort of service was in progress. From where they stood at the back of the crowd they could not see the preacher, but the rich Scottish accent left Tom in no doubt as to who was preaching. Scotch Will appeared to be almost at the end of his sermon and was speaking of some place where everything was light and joy and where all tears were gone for ever. Tom's mind immediately flashed back to Alice as she lay crying out in pain. Perhaps she had been taken to that land, he thought. But he knew he would never go there; he was too naughty, and anyway it sounded from what Scotch Will was saying that most people would not reach that beautiful place at all.

Under the scaffold

Then a further surprise awaited Tom. As Scotch Will finished his sermon the familiar sound of William Grimshaw's Yorkshire accent broke the silence. He was closing the gathering with prayer. Clearly he was no longer annoyed with William Darney's presence in his parish, and it even seemed that the curate was actually supporting him now. Had that secret meeting in the old quarries had something to do with it, Tom wondered? Quite obviously the people were also surprised to see their curate at Scotch Will's side.

No sooner had the last deep tones of the prayer died away, than a far different sound was heard. 'Mad Grimshaw is turned Scotch Will's clerk,' said a sneering voice. The words were taken up by another, and then another. Soon a large section of the crowd had joined in: 'Mad Grimshaw is turned Scotch Will's clerk... Mad Grimshaw is turned Scotch Will's clerk...' On and on they chanted and Tom, regardless of the newly-baked oatcakes Mrs Grimshaw had so recently given him, decided to join the fun. Louder and louder grew the refrain and even little George, taking courage from his older brother, added his piping voice to the chant: 'Mad Grimshaw is turned Scotch Will's clerk.'

The weather had suddenly become very cold as Tom and George turned to go home. A biting wind from across the moor chilled the afternoon air. But a greater chill rested on Tom's mind. He should never have mocked the man who had shown him nothing but kindness, as he had just done.

'Mad Grimshaw' was a term that many of the people had been using in secret to describe their new curate. Life in Haworth was hard, with scarcely a family that had not buried a father, mother or child in recent days. The desperate round of toil, poverty and hunger, in addition to the constant battle against the bitter climate in that village high in the Pennines, had produced a harshness among the people. Not more than a dozen Haworth villagers had been regular churchgoers before Grimshaw's arrival only eighteen months ago. Now the church was crowded. In fact there was only standing room for most of those who wished to attend. But the majority of men and women who crowded into St Michael's to hear Grimshaw's bold messages were not the locals. They came from outlying towns and villages and were often resented by the Haworth residents. Scotch Will had even made up a song about them. Tom could only remember a few lines, and that was because they were about pigs and their habits:

> There's many near the church that starve
> For want of Jesus' love.
> They do content themselves like swine
> To feed on husks and dirt.

The villagers also called their curate 'Mad Grimshaw' because they were never too sure what he was going to do next. He seemed to love playing tricks on people. They would tell each other the story of the day he had dressed up like a poor traveller with nowhere to spend the night. Pulling an old weaver's cap over his eyes, he had knocked on the door of a couple who had claimed to be very good Christians. Meekly he begged a bed for the night, giving every sign of being in a desperate situation. Angrily the couple tried to chase the 'beggar' from their door. When the curate removed his disguise he gave them a sermon on the sin of meanness which they would never forget.

Even worse than this, the curate would sometimes denounce the sins of his congregation in public, especially if he felt they were pretending to be something they were not and were living a life of lies. Little wonder then that many feared, even hated, him. Tom's father, Jack Whittaker, had his own story to tell. Instead of attending the church service as Grimshaw had so often urged him to do, he would frequently use the Sunday morning for a quiet drink in the *Black Bull*. It was against the law for taverns to remain open on a Sunday and Jack knew that. Just recently William Grimshaw had been in the habit of leaving the church while the congregation was singing the Psalm before the sermon and of marching into one of the three nearby public houses that stood in a ring around the church. If he found any of his parishioners inside, he would insist that they leave their beer glasses behind them and come into the church instead. Not many weeks earlier Jack had been relaxing in the *Black Bull* with his feet on the table and his glass in his hand. Suddenly another drinker shouted a warning, 'Mad Grimshaw's coming!' Dropping his half-empty glass to the ground, Jack leapt for the nearest window. Scrambling desperately through the narrow space he scaled a low wall and lay panting on the farther side. Had Mr Grimshaw seen him? Jack did not know, but he certainly had a sneaking suspicion that he may well have done.

When she could persuade Jack to stay at home and keep an eye on baby Molly, Mary Whittaker had occasionally attended the parish church, taking Margaret and a rather unwilling Tom along with her. The crush inside was so great at times that Mary and the children were obliged to perch on the gravestones outside the church. Grimshaw's loud penetrating voice carried through the open windows of the church, and they had little difficulty in hearing what he was saying. They understood that a letter had been written to the Archbishop in York, asking for permission to enlarge the church, complaining that 'the public worship of almighty God was greatly interrupted and disturbed by too crowding a congregation of people'. Privately Tom thought that if he did not have to go, it would help to ease the problem, but clearly his mother did not agree with him.

Tom had even heard that one man who lived six miles out of Haworth had a wife who refused to attend the services. One Sunday he dressed her in her best clothes and taking down a strong stick used it to beat her all the way from their farm to the church, just like an animal. She was apparently cursing and swearing all the way — Tom did not blame her when he heard that she was being beaten like that. Then he learnt that she was not swearing at her husband but was calling down curses on Mr Grimshaw instead, calling him 'that black devil' and other insulting names. But an amazing thing had happened. The next Sunday she came because she wanted to, and never missed a Sunday again. What had made such a difference, Tom was at a loss to explain. But of one thing he was sure, Mr Grimshaw cared very much about the people in the parish, whether they came to church or not. After he had preached a frightening sermon, all about hell, Tom had heard him say, 'Don't be angry with me, please don't. It is because I love you that I speak to you like this. Love will not let me see you perish.' That was certainly part of the reason why so many people came to hear Mr Grimshaw preach, but Tom guessed that there must be more to it than that.

5.
A cry on the moors

Tom was on lookout duty. He had been chosen to watch for the approach of the curate while his friends enjoyed a game of football on the moors. Not that Mr Grimshaw frowned on the village boys playing there — far from it. In fact quite often he would join in with them; but this was a Sunday afternoon. Again and again he had told the boys that Sunday was not the day for football on the moors. He had even spoken of his displeasure from the pulpit, but it made no difference. Tom and his friends would respond by looking for a new patch of ground where they could play without the curate knowing.

Mr Grimshaw had grown wise to their ways, however, and very often on a Sunday afternoon he had taken to strolling on the moors in search of the young footballers. And one could never tell when he might appear. Five-bar gates were no obstacle. Although he was now thirty-eight years of age, the curate seemed as agile as any youth. With a leap he would clear the gate and be on the scene even before the lookout boy had time to warn the others of his approach. And if they were caught, the boys knew well enough that their parents would be notified — and that meant trouble.

Two years had passed since Alice had died. It was now the summer of 1745. Tom had turned ten, George was nearly seven and thirteen-year-old Margaret was always hard at work with her mother, dyeing, combing, spinning the wool worsted on which the family depended for their livelihood. Haworth was second only in importance to Halifax for the worsted materials, woven from the wool of the long-haired sheep that grazed on the moors. At three and a half years of age Molly was no longer a baby: her ceaseless chatter and mischievous ways left the family with few dull moments.

Tom had spent almost two years at the village school and had made good progress. His reading was excellent although he found the writing harder. However, his education had stopped abruptly. Tall and strong, he was becoming such a great help to his father on the farm that Jack Whittaker felt unable to manage without him. Tom had been obliged to give up his place at the school and now spent the days working with his father instead. Jack had never learnt to read or write and to him such knowledge was hardly necessary for the life his son was likely to lead. Each morning Tom was employed in caring for the animals, planting and tending the vegetable crops; and in the afternoons he would sometimes accompany his father to market to buy in fresh raw materials or to sell his produce.

Often Tom roamed the moors, checking up on the condition of the sheep Jack owned. He knew each woolly, black-faced animal by name, and if he discovered a ewe that had hurt its leg or appeared to be sick, he would note its condition and report it to his father. Together they would return and Jack would carry the injured animal back home where he could tend it more easily. Tom loved the wide open spaces of the moors. He knew the hidden tracks and the secret valleys where moorland streams tumbled fiercely downwards. Here the water was pure and clean and the boy would lie flat on his face drinking deeply, before continuing his walks. The scent of the yellow gorse in the spring or the sight of the heather in the late summer that turned the hills into a sea of purple never failed to delight him. He recognized the calls of the moorland birds, the mournful cry of the lapwing, the sweet song of the lark. He knew too how suddenly the mists could come down blotting out every familiar landmark.

One afternoon in early October Tom had set out together with Tivvy the family dog to check on the condition of the sheep. The sun had been struggling all day to pierce the sea of damp cold mist, and at last it seemed to have won the battle. Whistling cheerfully as he climbed, Tom was not aware at first that the mist had returned and was growing ever denser, wrapping itself around every tree and shrub. Perhaps he ought to return home. Certainly he would not be able to see where the sheep were grazing. As he stood irresolute, he thought he heard a cry. It came from somewhere above him — from a place where he knew the ground dropped away sharply and suddenly. It was a place where large boulders lay strewn along the bottom of a small valley — as if some giant had been throwing them around in a fit of temper.

Yes, it was a cry — in fact it sounded like a child's cry. But how could a young child possibly be up on the moor in such weather? Groping his way forward for a few moments, he stumbled over something — something soft. As the sheep gave an indignant bleat and disappeared into the mist, Tom laughed to himself. It must have been a sheep that he had heard. But no! there it was again. A child was crying out somewhere in the cleft of the moors above him. Then an idea struck Tom. He whistled to Tivvy his border collie. 'Go Tiv, go find,' he commanded. The dog disappeared obediently into the mist. He seemed to know what Tom wanted. A few moments later he was back, barking, trotting forward and then returning.

Slowly Tom followed, placing his feet as carefully as possible to avoid slipping. Then he found himself at the top of the steep downward slope. Grasping bracken and branches of shrubs to steady himself, he gradually descended into the small valley. It was clearer as he neared the bottom — and then he saw her, only a few yards away. She seemed to be a dark-haired girl, perhaps about nine years of age, trapped by one foot between two great boulders. 'I'm coming,' Tom called, 'I'm coming.' Only as he approached the spot where the child lay did he recognize her. Jane Grimshaw! 'What's th' matter?' he cried in alarm. 'What yer doin' here?' A low moan was all the reply he received. Then he saw that Jane must have fallen down the side of the cleft, disturbing a boulder as she fell. It had rolled down on top of her, pinning the child's foot under its weight. Her ankle might be badly injured, even broken; Tom did not know.

Jane gazed at Tom with grateful, terrified eyes. Somehow he must move that boulder, he thought to himself, but it would not be easy. Summoning all his strength he pulled and tugged. Now the heavy boulder moved an inch, then another, then a little more. And then quite suddenly it gave way — so suddenly that Tom himself tumbled over, narrowly avoiding hitting his head on another boulder. 'Can yer stand?' he asked the girl. Jane tried, but fell back with a sharp cry. Clearly he was going to have to carry her down the moor.

Stooping down, he managed to gather her small frame in his arms. He began moving forward slowly, very slowly, following the line of the valley. Fortunately the stream had dried up as little rain had fallen during the summer and Tom knew the lie of the land well. Painstakingly he staggered down with his burden, thankful that Jane was not a heavy child. She was clinging to his neck, as if her life depended on it. Sometimes he had to sit down to rest for a few moments before struggling on. Tivvy went in front, wagging his tail and barking. He for one appeared to be enjoying the adventure. 'I prayed you'd come,' whispered Jane, looking up at Tom trustingly. Tom gave her a strange look in return. Perhaps that is what a parson's child is taught to say, he thought. But, then, if God had really sent him to help Jane, maybe he ought to listen to the things that Mr Grimshaw was saying in church a little more carefully.

The mist was clearing away as they reached the lower slopes. But Tom could hardly go on any further. Exhausted he sank down on a stone to rest. Just at that moment he heard the sound of another voice — calling out Jane's name. The voice was one he knew well. William Grimshaw was out searching for his child. She had left the house to pick heather on the moor earlier that afternoon and must have lost her way as the mist came down. 'O Tom, thank you, thank you,' cried the grateful father, taking Jane up in his strong arms.

'Do yer think she has hurt herself badly?' Tom enquired anxiously.

Under the scaffold

'I don't know,' replied her father, 'but her mother will soon put her to rights. You must come and see her, Tom, when she is better.'

Tom did not go to see Jane. He was too nervous about knocking on that great door again. Besides, he had not always been well behaved, and Mr Grimshaw might remember that only a few weeks ago he and his friends had been teasing the curate, running up behind him to see who could touch him without being seen. Quite suddenly Mr Grimshaw had turned round and given chase. And could he run! Tom was amazed. The curate caught up with one of his friends, William Hartley from the next farm. He picked him up as though he were a feather weight, and hung him on a nearby butcher's hook by his collar, while he set off after the next rascal. Tom was hiding behind a wall and could see everything. Will was going quite blue in the face before Mr Grimshaw came back and took him down. Will's mother, Jeanie, who was Mary Whittaker's friend, was upset and angry when she heard what had happened to her boy, which was not surprising. But it had been a warning to Tom and his friends, and certainly the boys had not teased Mr Grimshaw since then.

Tom had heard, however, that Jane was hobbling about the house again and that her ankle was only badly sprained and bruised, but not broken. But he did go to visit his old friend from higher up on the moor. Farmer Greenwood was always pleased to see Tom. Few people ever called on him, and most thought that the lonely old shepherd was a little mad. Perhaps living alone 'with the wind wutherin' round his small hut and nowt but sheep for company had done it', they suggested.

Tom told Mr Greenwood the whole story of how he had heard Jane crying out in the mist high up the moor, of how he had managed to climb down and move the boulder that was trapping her, and how he carried her back down the moor until they had met her father out looking for her. 'D' yer know what she said?' he enquired shyly. 'She said she'd prayed to God that I'd come. D' yer really think that's true, Mr Greenwood? Did God really send me? I prayed that my Alice would get better an' she never did.'

Farmer Greenwood was silent for a few moments. 'Maybe God meant something better than this world for your Alice,' he said at last. 'And Tom, I've bin thinkin' like. P'haps us both ought t' pay more heed t' what th' parson says. What d'yer say?' Tom did not say anything at all, but secretly he had to admit to himself that he had thought the same thing when Jane first said that she had been praying.

Not many weeks after this, Tom's mother Mary set off for the morning service at St Michael's, together with Tom and Margaret. Since Alice had died Mary had tried to be more regular in her attendance even though her poor clothes made her feel ashamed. Tom often glanced at his mother's face as she listened to Mr Grimshaw preaching. At times she looked so troubled that it worried Tom, but he was afraid to ask her why.

On this particular Sunday the family found a pew near the front of the church. From here Tom had a good view of the stained-glass windows and the massive pulpit in which Mr Grimshaw was standing. He could just read some of the words that ran all the way around the top of the pulpit. Some were long words, but he managed to figure them out: 'I am determined to know nothing among you save Jesus Christ...' Tom read. Then the words disappeared round the corner of the pulpit and he could not read them from where he was sitting. There were more words too, but he could not see them properly either: something about 'to live is Christ, and dying is gain'. Tom did not understand either set of words, but certainly the second was an idea he did not want to think about.

As Tom looked around the church, he suddenly caught sight of his friend old Farmer Greenwood sitting right in the front row. He was bending forward and seemed to be listening intently to everything Mr Grimshaw was saying. A stillness so deep that you could hear yourself breathe rested on the congregation. 'No matter how wicked you have been,' the preacher was saying, 'or how long you have neglected God, there is still mercy for you in Christ. There is still time to turn from your sins to the Saviour of sinners. He came for sinners like you...' Tom glanced across at Farmer Greenwood. To his amazement tears were streaming down the old farmer's furrowed, weather-beaten cheeks. Mr Grimshaw had seen it too. He leaned right over his big pulpit and addressed the old man personally: 'And for thee also, old moss-crop,'[1] he said with a depth of tenderness that Tom had rarely heard from him before.

Tom left the church that day in a sober frame of mind. He might be only a boy yet he knew that one day he too must ask God to forgive his sins. But for the moment he was not ready, and in any case, what would his gang of friends, Will Hartley, James Clayton and John Dene, say if they knew what he was thinking?

6.
The night of the storm

News of events of great national concern only reached Haworth when travellers happened to turn out of their way to visit friends in the village. So on the occasions when Tom Whittaker and his father travelled to Halifax or Bradford to sell their wool, pigs or other produce, the boy listened eagerly to the rumours passed from one to another in the market place. On a December day in 1745 Tom first heard of an invasion of the country that had begun earlier that year. Bonnie Prince Charlie, grandson of the last Stuart king, James II, had been trying to reclaim the English throne for the Stuarts, who had been replaced when George I of Hanover became king after the death of Queen Anne in 1714.

Tom learnt with astonishment of how the dashing young prince, with an army of Highlanders at his back, had inflicted a crushing defeat on the King's army of Redcoats at Prestonpans in Scotland during September. His imagination was stirred by descriptions of the Highlanders who, with their whoops and yells, their pitchforks, and scythes tied to the end of long poles, had surprised the Redcoats and sliced through their defences in little more than five minutes.

'Yeh,' added another, 'an' wi' aboot six thousand men Charlie got as far as Derby, he did. It were a close thing, that were.' The nearest they had come to Tom's village was to Preston, some thirty miles away. Such news stimulated and excited his boyish fancy. Perhaps one day he would leave Haworth and become a soldier. But as winter had set in he heard that the rebellion was all but over. The Young Pretender, as they called him, had been forced to retreat, first back to Carlisle and then to Scotland once more.

It was a bitter winter that year. As the wind howled around their home, the Whittaker family could often be found gathered in one room, huddled around the kitchen stove trying to keep warm. Snow had fallen early: Jack and Tom's wet clothes were regularly hung out to dry by the fire, creating a damp steam that turned to moisture and dripped slowly down the cold walls. But the animals still needed tending and feeding, and it appeared that a number of the ewes, now gathered in a field below the barn where the winter fodder was stored, might lamb early. As January turned to February, Jack watched the weather anxiously, for unless winter's icy grip gave way to milder weather soon, many of his lambs would die.

But by mid-February there was no sign of any let-up in the weather. Each morning Tom accompanied his father out into the unending whiteness of the snow-covered fields — the trees standing stark and black against the horizon. Although the sheep could root around for the coarse grass below the snow, they needed the fresh new hay from the barn if they were to lamb in safety. Tom scattered armfuls in the field and then turned his attention to the pigs, before hurrying indoors once more. His mother appeared far from well, and seemed to spend much of her time sitting by the fire. But when Mary told her family that she was expecting another baby in six months time, Tom had mixed feelings. What would his friends say? he wondered. But most of all he was a little anxious about his mother. At forty-three years of age, Mary would not find the birth at all easy, even though Margaret was a capable girl and had assured her mother that she would do all she could to help care for the new baby.

The barn where the hay was stored made an excellent place for Tom and his friends to chat together, free from the watchful eye of his older sister and his parents. With its warm musty smell it formed a shelter from the bitter weather beyond its doors. Tom was a popular figure among the other village boys; his inventive mind and cheerful spirit made him a natural leader. On many a winter afternoon his friends, Will, John and James, would gather in the Whittakers' barn where they enjoyed keeping warm by making dens for themselves among the bales. The sight of rats springing out of their winter beds as the bales were moved created much merriment among the boys. Eight-year-old George had begged to be able to join them but his request was firmly refused.

One bitter afternoon in late February the boys had collected in the barn once again. Outside a piercing north wind was whipping up the newly-fallen snow. It whistled through the cracks in the barn doors, and even a bed of hay could not shelter the boys from its chilling barbs. 'I say, Tom, how 'bout makin' a small fire in that there corner,' suggested James. 'It's right away from t'hay, and would soon warm us up.' Tom considered for a few moments. 'Yeh,' he said at length. 'I could get some coals from t' fire in t' kitchen, and we'd soon get this ol' place heated up.'

Without a second thought he disappeared towards the house, while James and Will set about gathering a few sticks together to lay a fire. Tom was soon back. The kitchen had been deserted and he had no difficulty in removing a few glowing embers from the fire with the shovel. Even better, there was still some bread on the table, and his hungry friends could now

53

enjoy an extra meal. The fire caught on quickly and the boys sat round, warming their frozen hands and feet and laughing. Tom kept a wary eye on the progress of the fire, to make sure that the flames did not flare out of control. Gradually they exhausted the supply of small sticks to feed the fire, and it began to peter out. Then quite unexpectedly John, the fourth and youngest member of the group, suddenly jumped up and grabbed a large armful of hay and threw it on the dying fire.

'John, yer great fool!' yelled Tom. But it was too late. In an instant the small fire sprang to life. Whipping off his coat, Tom began to beat frantically at the flames. At first it seemed he was succeeding, but a small tongue of flame had begun licking up the hay that lay on the floor around the fire. And now it had reached the nearest bale. With a roar the flames leapt out of control. There was nothing the boys could do. Knowing they were in serious trouble, Tom's three friends scattered to their homes. Certainly they did not want to take the blame for the loss of the Whittaker barn and all their winter supply of hay.

Tom gazed in desperate dismay. This was the worst thing he had ever done in his life and he did not dare to think what might happen to him. His coat had caught alight in the flames, and now there was little of it left. There was nothing to be done except to run for it himself, or he too could be trapped. But where could he run? He thought of old Farmer Greenwood — perhaps he could go there. Scarcely knowing what he was doing the boy rushed out into the freezing night, leaving the hay ablaze. A blizzard was beginning to rise, dashing the snow into Tom's eyes. At first he scarcely dared turn round to see what was happening to the barn. But when he did he saw the sky lit up as the flames rose into the night.

Tom struggled on. Now he was nearing Farmer Greenwood's cottage. He could just see a dim light in the window. But then he panicked. No, he could not go there. All his friend might do would be to insist that he went straight back home, and that he could not do. Turning his back on the inviting light he fought his way on, stumbling and slipping as he went. Without a coat Tom's arms and legs were freezing. Ice gathered on his eyebrows turning them to frozen lines above his eyes; even his very breath seemed to freeze as he gasped and grunted with the effort. Every landmark was now blotted out in the blizzard, and although Tom was familiar with each twist and turn of the moorland paths, he found himself quite lost. Only one thing spurred him on. He must get away from the sight and sound of that fire raging in the field next to his home.

Tom did not know how far he had walked, nor did he know where he was going — all he knew was that he must fight his way forward. What he did not realize was that his body temperature had become dangerously low. He had heard of people freezing to death on the moors, but still he plodded on. Now he was becoming sleepy — so sleepy. All he wanted at that moment was somewhere to lie down and go to sleep. His steps slowed down, his eyes grew heavier and heavier until he could hardly keep them open. Soon he could scarcely place one foot in front of another. If only he could find a sheltered spot where he could sleep and sleep. Perhaps he would wake up and find that it was all a dreadful dream.

At last he came to a place where a large boulder reared itself up in front of him. It would protect him from the icy blast of the wind that was gusting down from the heights of the moor above him. Thankfully Tom lay down, cupping his hands under his head to form a sort of pillow. And soon he drifted off to 'sleep'. In fact he had lost consciousness.

Meanwhile Farmer Greenwood was making a last-minute check on his sheep before bolting his door against the storm and settling down for the night. Throwing an extra cloak round his shoulders, he took down his storm lantern from its hook and lit it. Then with his strong stick in one hand and the lantern in the other, he opened his back door. Snow swirled in his face as he ventured out of doors. The sheep were huddled together for warmth against a long low boundary wall that ran beside his cottage. They would be all right for the night. But just as he turned to go back into the house, Farmer Greenwood noticed something on the far side of the wall that made the old man gasp with something between a choke and a cry.

Footsteps! Not far from where he was standing there were footsteps in the snow. The new snow was fast covering them from view, but without doubt someone had walked that way within the last hour or so. Whoever could it be? Examining the steps more carefully with the flickering light from his lantern, the farmer noticed that they were not a man's footsteps — no, they were too small for that. Some child had passed not far from his cottage. And if a child were out on the moors on a night like this he or she might well be dead by now.

'Who could it be?' the old man thought. Then in a flash he knew. 'Tom! It must be Tom! Who else could it possibly be?' Only a boy as impetuous as Tom would be stupid enough to venture out onto the moors on a night like this. Perhaps he had been in trouble yet again and escaped up to the moor. He must be out there somewhere in that terrible whirling blizzard. Every moment counted — the snow would soon fill in the tracks, hiding them from sight. Then Farmer Greenwood might never find him. Hurrying as fast as his old legs could carry him, the farmer opened his shed and took out his rough home-made sledge, which he used for carrying bales of hay across the snow. Only made of planks of wood nailed together, with a rope by which to pull it along, it had nevertheless proved invaluable in the past for hauling loads across the snow that were too heavy for him to manage alone.

Slowly, purposefully, the old man began to follow the footsteps, dragging his sledge along with him. Now the tracks were so faint that he could hardly see them at all. Snow blinded his eyes and the deafening roar of the wind carried his calls of 'Tom, Tom! Where are you?' far away as if the words were mocking him. Then he found the footsteps again, and always they were leading further and further up the moor. Several times Farmer Greenwood himself floundered where the ground became uneven or suddenly dropped away. Then he seemed to lose the tracks altogether. Perhaps he would pick them up again further on.

But no, he could see no further steps at all. He wandered all around peering anxiously this way and that for further traces of the boy's movements. Wherever could Tom have got to? Wearily he sat down on a boulder jutting out of the frozen waste to try to think what he ought to do. If he could not find the lad soon he would have to return to his cottage alone or there would be two deaths on the moors that night. As he sat he tried to blink away the tears that kept starting in his eyes. Then he noticed something he had not seen before. Not far from where he was sitting he thought he could see the tip of an old boot, sticking out of the snow. No! there were two boots. Jumping up from where he was sitting he began to scrabble wildly with his hands, and yes, it was Tom! The boy was lying unconscious under a light covering of snow, his body sunk into the soft whiteness beneath him as into a feather mattress. His face looked strangely peaceful, as though he were sleeping in his bed. But Farmer Greenwood was too experienced to think that Tom had merely fallen asleep.

Gradually he uncovered the boy's entire body. Bringing his sledge alongside, he pulled with all his remaining strength, and before long had managed to roll Tom onto it. He listened carefully to see if he could hear him breathing, but the wind was too loud. Stripping off the extra coat that he had put on to protect himself against the storm, he wrapped it round the motionless form and set off as quickly as he could towards his cottage, dragging his precious load behind him.

At last Farmer Greenwood reached his own front door. He was now on the point of collapse himself. Only the intense desire to save Tom's life if at all possible had driven him onward. In one last effort he managed to lift his young friend off the sledge and staggered inside with him. He laid his burden down as gently as he could beside the dying embers of his fire. Tom was so still, so white, that at first the old man feared he might be too late already. But as he listened carefully Farmer Greenwood felt sure he could catch the sound of very shallow breathing. After a moment or two to recover from his own exhaustion, and with a new sense of hope, the farmer warmed some old rags, holding them near the fire. With these he began to gently rub the boy's frozen hands and feet. On and on he worked. Then he prepared a little warm goat's milk and putting some on a spoon tried to force it through Tom's closed lips. Most seemed to run down the side of his cheek, but not all. He must continue trying. Was he imagining it, or was there really a tinge of colour creeping back into Tom's pale face?

The moments crept by like hours as the farmer re-warmed his clothes and kept massaging Tom's cold limbs. He had sometimes revived his frozen lambs in this way and knew he must not give up. Quite suddenly Tom gave a sigh. 'Yes!' Farmer Greenwood thought with a thrill of excitement, 'He's going to live!' Then equally suddenly Tom sneezed and opened his eyes. 'Where am I?' he murmured. 'Yer safe w' me,' answered the old man. Then with another sigh Tom turned over and fell asleep. This time

it was a natural sleep. Farmer Greenwood knew he could not contact Tom's parents that night, nor would it be safe to move the boy again. Stoking up the fire to keep the room warm, he covered him up and went to bed.

Farmer Greenwood was awake early the next morning. The storm had passed. A strange unearthly stillness had taken its place. The fields stretched away into the distance in crisp unbroken whiteness. Creeping quietly down the kitchen, the farmer looked carefully at Tom. He was still asleep but his cheeks were now a natural healthy colour. Without waiting to eat, the kindly old man threw a coat round his shoulders and stepped out into the new snow, his feet sinking in deeply. Before long he was standing at the door of Old Acre Farm. Then he looked across the field. There he saw the ruins of the family barn, burnt to the ground with only the framework remaining, standing like a strange black skeleton. Now he understood.

Jack Whittaker came to the door. His drawn anxious face spoke for itself. 'I've got your boy,' said Greenwood simply.

Under the scaffold

Without waiting for a word of explanation, Jack grabbed his coat and was striding up towards the farmer's cottage. Farmer Greenwood struggled to keep up with him. When Jack reached the door he waited for the breathless old man to catch up, and together they entered the small kitchen. Tom was awake now. He stretched out his arms towards his father. 'Pa, I'm sorry,' was all he said. 'Tom, m' boy,' said Jack, the tears streaming down his face, 'yer safe, nowt else matters.' The barn, burnt to cinders, and the loss of all his winter's hay seemed of little importance compared with his boy.

As Farmer Greenwood brewed a cup of tea for them all, he told Jack the story from his point of view. Tom said nothing. Clearly any explanations from him would have to come later. Picking up his son in his strong arms, Jack carried Tom to the door. 'One day I'll be back t' thank yer properly,' he said hoarsely as he turned to go.

7.
A prayer God heard

Jack Whittaker carried Tom all the way back to Old Acre Farm. Tom was a tall boy and even though his father was strong, he did not find it easy going as his feet sank deep into the new snow at every step. Without a word to Mary he struggled up the narrow stairs of his home with his burden and laid Tom on his bed. 'Thanks Pa,' Tom whispered and in a few moments was fast asleep once more.

When Tom woke, his mother was sitting by his bedside with a bowl full of porridge. The dark lines under her eyes told of her sleepless night. Old Acre Farm stood at a distance from the village and though the spire of flames and the black plume of smoke had been clearly visible against the leaden night sky, by the time any of the neighbours had managed to make their way through the storm it was too late to save the barn. But where was Tom? No one seemed to know. The flames were too intense for anyone to approach the inferno. The general opinion seemed to be that perhaps he was hiding and would turn up soon.

However, Jack and Mary Whittaker knew their boy better than that — they knew how reckless he was, how he acted with no regard to consequences... They could only come to one dreadful conclusion: Tom had been trapped inside the barn as he had stayed to try and beat out the flames and must have perished. As the fire subsided enough for Jack to rake through the ashes, the discovery of the remains of Tom's charred coat offered little consolation. While Jack continued to search the outhouses, Mary sat beside the dying kitchen fire. George and Molly were upstairs asleep. Margaret had stayed with her mother for a while, but there was nothing anyone could say or do. Eventually she too went to bed, leaving Mary alone.

For many months Mary had been deeply disturbed by the sermons she heard from the curate, William Grimshaw. How often he warned the people to seek the forgiveness of their sins before it was too late. Death came early to the people of Haworth and at forty-three Mary had already had more years than most. But it was not that Mary was unwilling to recognize her sins. That was not her problem. Her fear was that even if she did ask God for his forgiveness for the sake of his Son, her prayer would return unheard, for she had neglected God for too long — and such neglect, she had heard Mr Grimshaw say, was the greatest sin of all. If only God would give her some sign that he would not turn her away. Then she might pluck up courage to ask him for mercy and forgiveness. As she sat by the fire that night the thought of her son's plight and her own need became so desperate that at last she offered up a broken prayer. 'Lord, if somehow you can save my Tom, then I will know that you are willing to hear the cries of even a poor woman like me.'

And God *had* heard her cry. Tom was safe and it looked as if he would recover. 'I prayed that God would save your life, Tom,' his mother said quietly, as she handed Tom the bowl of porridge. Tom gave a jump, and looked hard at his mother. That was just like what Jane Grimshaw had said when he found her on the moors that time. But to hear his own mother saying it was quite different. For the first time in his life the eleven-year-old began to wonder about his own sins. However, for the moment he was still feeling a little dizzy and light-headed. So he just nodded, ate up his porridge gratefully and fell back to sleep.

From that day onwards Mary Whittaker could always be found at St Michael's on a Sunday morning. Even when her pregnancy was far advanced her place was seldom empty. Nor was it easy for her to sit through a two-hour sermon on the hard wooden pews. But the moments passed by so quickly that she lost all awareness of time. Her whole mind was absorbed in listening to Mr Grimshaw preaching. The church was still packed to the corners with men and women anxious to hear what the curate had to say. Tom had heard that some people even walked from as far away as twenty miles each Sunday to hear the preaching. Realizing his sermons were too long, Mr Grimshaw had once explained, 'I can scarcely tell how to leave off, lest I omit something that might bring your souls to salvation.' And still the people sat rooted to their seats, listening intently.

But not so Tom Whittaker. Every now and then his sister Margaret turned to glower at him as he began to fidget around. At times Mr Grimshaw looked in his direction and it almost seemed as if he were about to stop and address the restless boy from the pulpit. However, when a dog fight broke out in church (for many parishioners brought their animals with them), Tom could hardly stop laughing. After the two owners had failed to separate the snarling animals, Mr Grimshaw had boomed out in his deep voice, 'What! Have you no feet?' and then actually demonstrated what he meant by lifting one of the dogs high in the air with his sturdy boot as he crossed from the lectern to the pulpit. Tom chuckled endlessly over that all the way home.

On another occasion the curate had sent two of his church wardens out during the Psalm before the sermon to check up on parishioners drinking in the *White Lion Inn*. When the wardens did not return Mr Grimshaw left the church himself to see what had happened. Tom waited breathlessly, only too glad that his own father had gone to the Bradford market that day and would not be caught. Then he heard Mr Grimshaw coming. Tom recognized his heavy tread immediately. And in front of him came the wardens, walking with heads down like two naughty schoolboys. 'What think ye? What think ye?' thundered the curate. 'Those whom I sent out to detect others and prevent them from sinning, I have found in the inn drinking a pint of ale themselves! For shame! For shame! For shame!' These last words were repeated three times over as he slowly mounted his pulpit once more. Certainly, thought Tom to himself, you could never be sure just what Mr Grimshaw might do next. He could not help stealing a glance across at Jane and John Grimshaw as they sat with their mother in the family pew. Quite clearly they too thought it was very funny, and John's face was twisted into an odd shape as he tried not to laugh out loud.

As the icy grip of winter slowly released its hold, Jack Whittaker set about rebuilding his barn with Tom's help. Tom had never told his father that it was his friend James who had suggested lighting the fire, or that John had thrown on the armful of hay that had sent it out of control. He had allowed his father to think that the fault was entirely his. Tom might be reckless and foolish at times but he was absolutely loyal to his friends and they knew it.

Robert Hartley, who rented nearby Meadow Head Farm and whose son Will was one of Tom's gang, had been most generous to the family, giving spare bales of hay to help Jack until he was able to take his animals out to pasture once more. He may well have guessed that his son could have been involved in the disaster. By March the lambing season was in full swing. Tom was becoming quite expert at helping his father with the ewes when there was a difficult birth or even when twins or triplets were born. He never failed to be amazed when a tiny newborn lamb emerged into the world. After its mother had licked it clean, it would stagger onto its thin wobbly legs and bleat pathetically as it tried to keep up with its mother and steal an extra drink or two. The sows were in litter too, but Tom did not find them so attractive.

Although he was kept busy, there was still time to visit his friend Farmer Greenwood or walk on the moors, clambering on the rocks, listening to the birds singing and looking for the first spring flowers. The old farmer had not been so well since the night he had rescued Tom. He was breathing badly and coughed a great deal. Tom felt guilty about it, though his friend did not seem sad. Instead he talked to Tom quite a lot about heaven, and even appeared to be looking forward to being there. 'Death will let me into a better world and bring me into the arms of my Saviour,' he told Tom on one occasion. Tom remembered hearing Mr Grimshaw say something very similar. But for Tom himself death was a frightening thing and he tried hard not to think about it.

The months passed quickly. Tom still joined his friends for games of football on the moor, taking care that Mr Grimshaw did not discover them if they were playing on a Sunday. Occasionally Tom caught sight of Jane Grimshaw as she was out shopping with her stepmother or taking a gift to some neighbour in need. She seemed a serious girl, although she always appeared glad to see Tom and would smile shyly at him. Tom found himself wishing he could get to know her better, but the thought of knocking on the curate's front door soon made him think that he had better not try.

The day that Mary Whittaker's baby was due was fast approaching. But Tom was still troubled about his mother. She seemed so tired, and although that anxious look had gone, Tom realized that she was not very well. Then one night in August as he was almost asleep, his father suddenly burst into his room. 'Tom, Tom, go quick and fetch the midwife. Haste ye, boy, there aint no time t'lose.' Throwing on a few clothes Tom raced down to the village and hammered on the door of the local midwife. Grumbling and panting, the middle-aged woman, a little overweight and out of condition, followed Tom up the hill and out along the moonlit road.

Tom crept back to his bed, but not to sleep. Doors banged and voices sounded not far from his room. Then, just after the Haworth church clock had struck midnight, he heard a sound he had never heard before: a thin high-pitched wail — and then nothing. Clearly the baby had arrived and Tom's presence would not be wanted at that moment, so he turned over and soon drifted off to sleep. When he woke the next morning Tom slipped into his mother's room. She turned her head as he entered. She looked so tired, but ran her fingers lovingly through his hair. 'Tom,' she said in a low voice, 'yer have a new little sister.' She hesitated for a moment and then said, 'Yer can pick her up, Tom, if yer like.' Tom crossed to the crib and looked down at the tiny face, so wrinkled and red, a contrast with her mop of black hair. The baby was awake and her deep blue eyes seemed to be looking far beyond him. Picking her up cautiously, Tom stroked his new sister's soft cheek with his finger. 'What we callin' her, Ma?' he asked at last. 'We want to call her Jane, like Mr Grimshaw's girl,' answered his mother. 'But Tom,' and her voice faltered, 'the midwife don't think we're goin' to keep her. She says she aint breathin' proper, and she don't know what's wrong.'

Tom was speechless. He laid the baby gently back in her crib, and sat down beside his mother for a little while. Then quite suddenly he jumped up and left the room, and before many moments had passed he was climbing up to the moors just as he had done before Alice had died. He needed to be alone; he always needed to be alone when he was in trouble. By the time he returned, baby Jane's frail spirit had gone; her few short hours of life were over.

The fact that so many Haworth infants died made it no easier for the family. Jack dealt with his pain in the only way he knew, by spending longer hours at the *Black Bull*. Even Molly and George seemed sad. Margaret was so busy caring for her mother that she had little time to speak to Tom. Where had that baby's spirit gone? he wondered. Perhaps Farmer Greenwood could tell him. So Tom climbed up to the old man's cottage and told him all about the way his new baby sister had died the very same day that she was born. His friend was sympathetic, but he was far from well himself; his cough made it hard for him to talk so Tom did not stay long.

As the days passed, a yet greater trouble hovered over the Whittaker family. Mary was not regaining strength. She seemed so weak, and had no appetite for the small dishes that Margaret was cooking for her. On the fifth day after the birth of the baby her temperature began to rise. The midwife called back to see her, and declared that Mary was suffering from childbed fever — words that every mother dreaded to hear — and Mary was only too aware that they meant that she would probably be taken from her young family. Even if he had been able to afford the medicines available, Jack Whittaker knew that little could be done for that condition. Tom found his father alone in the cowshed that afternoon, his head leaning against the cow's warm flank. 'O Tom, what am I goin' t'do without her?' was all he could say as his older son entered the shed.

The next day Tom found himself alone with his mother. Jack was out digging up the onions and George was with him. Margaret was in the kitchen spinning and keeping an eye on Molly. Mary appeared to be asleep. She looked feverish and flushed. 'Ma, Ma, don't die, please don't,' Tom whispered desperately, half to himself. Quite suddenly he seemed to hear again his mother's voice as she had sat by his bed after Farmer Greenwood had rescued him on the night of the fire: 'I prayed that God would save your life, Tom.' Those were her exact words, and God had heard her prayer. Suppose he tried praying that God would save his mother's life. The family needed her so badly... Molly was only four... But would God possibly hear the prayer of a boy who always fidgeted in church, quite often told lies to get out of trouble and played football on Sundays? He did not know. But Farmer Greenwood had told him that God had heard him when he prayed even though he had done a lot of wrong things in his life. With all the earnestness he could command, Tom Whittaker prayed that God would come and heal his mother. He could not promise to be good — he knew he would not keep his promise, but at that moment he felt a strange longing in his heart to please and love God in the same way that his mother and Farmer Greenwood did.

Mary was no worse by the evening. In fact it was just possible to imagine that she was a little better. She had squeezed Tom's hand and told him to be a good boy and to be helpful to his Pa and to Margaret, and to be kind to George. She even managed a spoonful or two of soup that Margaret had prepared. By the next day there was no doubt about it. Her fever was not so high. Even the midwife seemed surprised that she was still alive and told her that she might get better. During the days that followed, Tom's mother gradually, very gradually, gained strength. God had heard and answered the prayer of a twelve-year-old boy.

8.
A kindness repaid

Haworth was agog with excitement. It was late October in 1746 and a visitor had been seen riding up Main Street, his sturdy horse struggling from time to time as its hooves slipped on the steep uneven flagstones.[1] He had stopped to ask one of the villagers the way to Mr Grimshaw's home. Who was the stranger? Everyone wanted to know. Visitors were rare in the village, apart from those who came on a Sunday to hear Mr Grimshaw preach; such news spread quickly from one to the other. Someone who had just been visiting relatives in nearby Keighley, however, seemed to have the answer. 'It's One-of-the-Wesleys,' he announced in a knowing sort of voice, adding by way of explanation, 'he is a travelling preacher a bit like Scotch Will, and he is on his way to Newcastle. He stayed at Keighley overnight and he preached to the people there. He taught them how to sing some wonderful words; some people even said he had written them himself.'

Tom Whittaker had been about to set off for the village to collect the water when he saw the stranger coming. Approaching Old Acre Farm he had reined in his horse and asked Tom if he was still on the right road for Sowdens. As Tom pointed out the track ahead, he noticed that the visitor was wearing a clerical gown with two white tabs round his neck just like Mr Grimshaw, and he too wore a wig. Perhaps he is another vicar, thought Tom as he stared after the distinguished-looking horseman. He seemed to Tom to be quite a short man, and the boy noticed particularly his sharp bright-looking eyes and fine straight nose. By his mud-bespattered gown, it looked as if he had been on the road for a long time.

Tom was just about to return home after drawing his water when he saw the same man cantering back along West Lane. He had learnt from the crowd that gathered near the pump that the visitor was called One-of-the-Wesleys — a very odd name thought Tom to himself. As he approached Head Well, the stranger dismounted, declaring, 'My name is Charles Wesley, and I bring you heavy tidings. I have to tell you that both your curate and his wife are seriously ill.' A gasp arose from the people, as Charles Wesley spoke further: 'I fear greatly that God may take them away from you, and take Mr Grimshaw from the service of his church. But,' he continued, 'I prayed with him that God might raise him up again, and I may tell you that his soul is filled with triumphant love. I could have wished mine in its place.' A murmur broke out among the listening people, as Charles Wesley climbed up on some nearby steps and announced that he would preach to them. His text was 'Say to them that are of a fearful heart, Be strong, fear not… [God] will come and save you'.[2] Many people were crying as they listened, some because of Mr

Wesley's words, but mostly because of the thought that their curate might die.

Tom could only think of Jane Grimshaw. Whatever would happen to John and to Jane if their parents died. Mr Wesley had also added something about Jane's stepmother. Everyone in Haworth knew that Elizabeth Grimshaw had been of no help to her husband in his preaching. In fact, she had made it as difficult for him as she possibly could and had quite often openly opposed him as well. Even so, Tom liked Jane's stepmother. She had always spoken kindly to him and particularly after he had carried Jane down from the moor when she had hurt her ankle. But now Mr Wesley told the people something else. He told them that a great change had come to Mrs Grimshaw, and just like Tom's own mother Mary she had become a quite different person as she had found forgiveness for her sins through the Lord Jesus Christ. The listening crowd scarcely knew whether to be glad or sad at all this news. After preaching to the people, Charles Wesley remounted his horse and rode off back to Keighley where he was due to preach that night.

Picking up his buckets of water, Tom made his way slowly home, but he was not thinking about anything else much except the news he had just heard of Jane's parents. How could the preacher really say, 'Be strong, fear not' when people you love are likely to die? he wondered. He remembered how he had felt as he had sat beside his mother only two months ago. Not many more days passed before the people of Haworth heard the sad news that Elizabeth Grimshaw had indeed died. They were greatly relieved to hear that their curate was much recovered — but how would he manage without Elizabeth to care for his children?

Two days later the funeral cortege passed Old Acre Farm. They were taking Elizabeth Grimshaw's body to the nearby village of

Heptonstall to bury her. Her home had been there before she married William Grimshaw five years earlier. Tom stayed out of the way, but from the window of the farm he could see the coffin slung on poles, being carried slowly over the rough track by four men from the village. Tom caught a glimpse of John and Jane following the coffin. Jane's face looked so white and sad. Tom fought back his tears. How easily it could have been him following a coffin if his mother had not recovered after the death of baby Jane.

Each Sunday as Tom, Margaret and sometimes even George attended the service at St Michael's with their mother, Tom used to think how lonely Mr Grimshaw looked. John and Jane sat in the pew on their own now, although sometimes Mol, the new housekeeper at Sowdens, would sit with them. A warm-hearted fussy old woman, she did her best to make sure the curate ate his meals properly and that he kept warm as he set off to preach in distant villages across the moors. Grimshaw had been known to give away his only coat if he came across some poor man who appeared colder than he was. Often Mol was in despair. She tried to care for Jane and John as well, but John, who was eleven and a half now, was not pleased at having Mol around the house. One Sunday the family pew was empty. Tom learnt that John and Jane had been sent to stay with their grandparents at Ewood, some twelve miles away. Tom was sorry about that because he had grown fond of Jane and realized that he might not see her again.

Winter nights were drawing in and there was not so much to do at the farm. Quite often Tom climbed up to see Farmer Greenwood, and the old man was always pleased to welcome him. He would stoke up his fire when Tom arrived and search round the kitchen for some small treat for a hungry boy. A strange pair they looked as they sat and chatted: about the moors, about the sheep, about the night of the fire. Tom had told his old friend about his secret prayer for his mother and how God had made her well again. He had been too shy to tell anyone else, but Farmer Greenwood seemed to understand and he had encouraged Tom to go on praying to God about his problems and needs. 'Tha maun [must] go on, m'boy. Don't yer be like me, that niver prayed to God till I were an ol' man,' he had warned.

Yet Tom was growing concerned about his friend. His cough was getting no better — in fact it was worse. Sometimes he seemed almost too tired to talk to Tom and he was losing weight as well. His rough old shepherd's coat hung loosely from his shoulders and his trousers were much more baggy than they used to be. Perhaps he is not eating properly, thought Tom. But when he arrived late one afternoon, he found his friend lying on his bed, his dinner untouched upon the table. Tom knew that something was seriously wrong. That night he talked to his father about it. 'I wish we could do some'at for ol' Farmer Greenwood,' he said, 'I'm sure he's sick.'

Jack said little to Tom, but later when Tom was in bed he discussed what his son had said with Mary. She had grown much stronger again and so when Jack suggested that they might ask the old man to stay with them until he was a little better, she readily agreed. Jack had not forgotten his promise to repay the debt they owed to the farmer for risking his own life to save Tom. When Jack went to his cottage to make the suggestion, Farmer Greenwood was reluctant to come. Who would care for his sheep? he had asked. 'Why, Tom would be glad to,' responded Jack, 'there aint nowt our Tom don't know about sheep these days.' And so arrangements were made to bring the farmer down to Old Acre for a while. Tom agreed to sleep in the loft, even though it was dark and airless up there at night, so that his friend could have his bed.

Under the scaffold

At first Farmer Greenwood used to sit by the fire in the kitchen and even took Molly on his lap and told her stories. George too loved to hear about the things Mr Greenwood had done when he was a small boy of seven. But the farmer was growing weaker each day in spite of the meals that Mary cooked for him. Mr Grimshaw often came in on his way from Sowdens Farm to the church. He would talk to the old man about heaven. Once Tom heard him say that for the Christian death should be no more frightening than going to your bed at night. 'A Christian makes no more of dying than when he is weary of falling asleep,' he said. Tom did not agree with him about that. For him death was a terrible thing, taking away the people you loved most. Yet Mr Grimshaw had lost Jane's own mother Sarah, and now Elizabeth, so he must know what he is talking about, he decided.

Before very long Farmer Greenwood stayed in his bed all day, and Tom realized that soon he would have to say goodbye to his friend for ever. One morning Tom slipped into the room to see the sick man before going off up the moors to round up the sheep and bring them down to the lower fields before the heavy snows set in. He wanted to know whether Farmer Greenwood would like him to bring his sheep down as well. 'Aye, m'boy, aye, I thank 'ee for that,' replied his friend. Then Tom noticed a strange look on the old man's face, almost as if he had just seen something very beautiful. 'Tom, lad, I have some'at to tell thee.' Tom remained rooted to the spot as Mr Greenwood continued: 'My Saviour stood by me last night. He stood right there where you be standin' now.' Tom looked a little frightened. Perhaps the old man was rambling because he was so ill. 'Aye, and d'yer know what he said t' me? He jest held out his arms like and said, "Come to me, and I will give you rest." That's all, Tom, but it were enough for an ol' man like me. Yer see, I've bin that tired lately; tired of m' sins, tired of m' coughin', tired o't' pain in m' chest, tired of all but thinkin' about him and about that rest he said about.'

Tom hardly knew what to answer. Eventually he asked, 'And what did yer say?'

'Me? Why I jest said, "I'm comin', Lord." And, Tom lad, it would be grand t'see tha agin one day up there.' Tom could bear no more and hurried from the room. When he arrived home that night, driving the sheep carefully in front of him with the help of Tivvy, the border collie, he learnt that his old friend had died not long after he had left to go up to the moors. But in Tom's mind it was not really death. No, he had just obeyed the call of the one who had said 'Come to me.'

9.
A riot at Roughlee

Almost a year had passed since the death of Farmer Greenwood. Tom often thought about him: it was not so much anything that his friend used to say that Tom missed, but the silent understanding that had grown up between them. Whenever he was in trouble Tom knew that the old shepherd was happy for him to sit by his fire until he felt able to go home once more.

Tom was now nearly thirteen years of age and fast approaching the time when most boys left home to become apprenticed to some trade. Jack Whittaker had considered the various options open to his older son. A friend of Jack's in Heptonstall was willing to take Tom as an apprentice to learn the skills of a wheelwright; the ability to manufacture wheels successfully, whether for carriages or for carts, was one that took a considerable time to learn. The spokes, rim, hub, all had to be measured accurately and balanced with the right degree of tension and precision. Such skills were a closely guarded secret of the trade. Alternatively, Tom could join Jake Bradshaw in his smithy to learn the art of making horse shoes, agricultural implements and household goods from iron. But the thought of a boy who loved an outdoor life and the wide spaces of sky and moor stooping over an anvil all his life was one that Jack

Whittaker quickly dismissed. The truth of the matter was that Tom was increasingly useful to Jack on the farm and his father was loathe to be without him. In any case, he argued, if Tom could expand the farm and perhaps add cattle to the pigs and sheep that Jack already bred and sold, that would make an excellent living for his older son. George could perhaps join him in due course for he too was showing the same interest in the farm.

Tom had seen little of Jane and John Grimshaw since their stepmother had died. He heard that John was causing his father many worries, and his elderly grandparents were also having trouble with him. One problem, so it was rumoured, was that the Grimshaw children were both due to inherit a lot of money when they reached the age of twenty-one. Their mother Sarah had been a Lockwood before her marriage and came from a well-to-do family. Although William Grimshaw himself was often in financial difficulties, no help came to him from his first wife's parents; all their money had been settled on Sarah's children instead. Knowing that he had a sizeable inheritance coming to him one day, John Grimshaw was lazy and difficult. Jane, on the other hand, so Tom had been told, had been much affected by the death of her stepmother. It had made her think deeply about her sins. Her father had recently said to a friend, 'For the last six months, my own little girl, between ten and eleven years of age, has begun to show a serious concern for her sinful state.' This puzzled Tom, for although he knew he had done plenty of wrong things and certainly needed to be sorry for his sins, Jane had always seemed so gentle, so even-tempered. He could not understand how she had much to worry about.

Hundreds still flocked into Haworth each Sunday to listen to William Grimshaw's preaching. Whenever Mary Whittaker could afford it she would invite people from a distance to come back to Old Acre for something to eat, even if it could only be onions boiled in whey, before starting on their journey home, either walking or on horseback. Jack would grumble in a good-natured way whenever this happened and would disappear for an hour or two until he was sure the visitors had gone. Mary had the good sense not to ask where he had gone, but she had a fair idea.

Tom had heard that the vicar in nearby Colne — George White by name — who had been in prison several times for debt due to his excessive drinking was becoming increasingly angry about the people from his parish travelling across the hills to hear his neighbour's preaching. He was even angrier when Grimshaw himself actually had the impudence to come into his parish to preach. Recently, so the village gossips said, White had threatened that if ever Grimshaw, or any of his friends such as Scotch Will, came into his parish again he would 'sacrifice ye last drop of blood to root 'em out'.

There was already trouble in the air when a visitor cantered into Haworth one August morning in 1748. Tom felt sure that he had seen the newcomer before, but then he realized that it must have been his brother whom he had seen. This was Mr John Wesley, Tom learnt, who together with his brother Charles had been preaching up and down the country. Wherever a group of men and women responded to the preaching of the brothers, or to that of the other preachers who worked with them, Mr Wesley would gather them together into small groups called Societies. His preachers would visit these Societies from time to time. Beyond that, Tom was not really interested in what the Wesley brothers were doing.

But now the whole village was astir with the news that John Wesley himself had arrived. Some had seen him when he paid an earlier visit the previous year, but for many this was the first chance to glimpse the man who had apparently created such a commotion in other parts of the country. Often there were mob riots when the Wesley brothers preached in the towns and villages. Houses were set on fire, men and women violently assaulted and sometimes even seriously hurt. Tom had heard that Mr Wesley himself had been injured by an angry mob when he was preaching at the Market Cross in nearby Halifax not many days earlier.

Word soon spread around the village of Haworth that Mr John, as many were calling him, was going to preach in the parish church at five o'clock that evening even though it was not a Sunday. Tom was a little bored that day and so decided that he would go along to see if the preacher was anything like Mr Grimshaw in the way he spoke. The resemblance between Mr John and his brother was unmistakable: both were small men, both had the same sharp blue eyes, the same prominent nose, but Mr

John's high cheekbones and firm mouth gave him the look of some army commander, or so Tom thought. Nor was the boy slow to notice that right across one cheek the preacher had an ugly red gash where a sharp stone had hit him right in the face. The Halifax mob had hurled a hail of mud, bricks and dirt at Wesley, but not until the blood was streaming down his cheek did he stop preaching. Even

John Wesley

then he had continued his sermon outside the town. Tom, who always felt strongly about everything, admired such courage but it made him very angry to think that the people of Halifax had acted so wickedly to one who had done them no harm.

The following day Tom heard that Mr Grimshaw and Mr Wesley were going to ride across to the village of Roughlee to preach. Roughlee was not far from Colne, and came into George White's parish, so the preachers were taking a risk in venturing into the area. 'There'll be trouble, ye mark my words,' the people of Haworth said to each other. Rumour had it that George White was raising what he called an 'army of protesters in defence of the Church of England'. He was to be 'commander-in-chief' and was promising a free pint of ale for each man who enlisted in his 'army' — an incentive to ensure that his 'soldiers' were sufficiently unruly and excited to attack the preachers fiercely. Added to this, they were to be provided with other 'proper encouragements'; these would include cudgels, stout sticks and stones. White determined that this 'army', or more accurately, drunken rabble, should assault the preachers and deal with them so brutally that it would prevent them from ever attempting to preach in his parish again.

Despite such rumours of trouble ahead and many urgent warnings, Mr Grimshaw and Mr Wesley set out early the next morning. It was a ten-mile trek on horseback across Haworth Moor, Keighley Moor, through the Forest of Trawden and finally, skirting around Colne, into the village of Roughlee where many were eagerly waiting to hear the preaching. They hoped that by going early John Wesley might be able to address the people and then leave immediately to return to Haworth before George White and his mob arrived on the scene. Several other friends from nearby Keighley were joining them at Roughlee to add their support for the preachers, including Thomas Colbeck, who kept a grocer's shop and was well known to the people of Haworth.

'What if Mr Grimshaw gets hurt like Mr Wesley?' Tom asked his mother anxiously.

'Mr Grimshaw's a big man,' she had answered. 'I guess he'd be a match for t'best of that vicar's army.'

Secretly, however, Tom had another plan in his mind. With little to do on the farm that hot August day, he made a reckless decision. Without weighing up the consequences, as was so often the case with Tom's ideas, he determined that he and his friends would go along as well. Perhaps a rival gang of youths from Colne, well known to Tom from their past scuffles, would be around. They will soon wish they had stayed at home, thought Tom savagely. Who could tell? Perhaps his gang could rescue Mr Grimshaw and his friend from George White's army. Gathering together in the new barn at Old Acre Farm, Tom's friends — James Clayton, Will Hartley, John Dene and a new member of the gang, Bob Bradshaw the blacksmith's son, whom they called Big Bob because of his size — were all eager to join him. They soon set off following the men on horseback at a distance, taking with them some bread to eat on the way.

The walk took the boys well over three hours, though for part of the way they managed to beg a lift from a farmer who was returning to Winewall, not far from Colne, with an empty cart after selling his goods in Keighley. Shortly after midday they reached the outskirts of Roughlee. Just at that moment they caught a glimpse of hordes of men waving sticks, staves and cudgels, yelling as they streamed down the hill from Colne into the village. The noise was frightening and was growing ever louder as the mob drew closer. The boys quickly hid behind an old barn until it had passed. They did not feel quite so brave now.

A riot at Roughlee

Arriving eventually at the edge of the crowd that had been listening intently to the preacher, Tom was aghast at what he saw. The 'army' had broken through and one big man who called himself the 'captain' was dragging Mr Wesley away. Scarcely had he agreed to go with the captain before another 'soldier', inflamed with alcohol and armed with a heavy stick, began to strike Mr Wesley on the head, not once but time and time again. As the preacher tried to protect himself with his hands, he stumbled and fell to the ground. Just as he managed to get back on his feet he was struck again and yet again. Tom saw Mr Grimshaw rush to his help and was using his sturdy boots to kick Mr Wesley's assailant. At last the man stopped. Then Tom saw the preacher being hauled off in the direction of Barrowford, a village almost a mile away. Apparently the local constable was waiting for him there at the *White Bear Inn*. He would 'examine' the preacher and pronounce judgement on Mr Wesley and Mr Grimshaw. But the constable was under orders from George White and had been told that no one was to be freed until a promise had been extracted from Mr Wesley that neither he, nor Grimshaw, nor any other Methodist preacher, would ever return to Colne parish to preach.

Surrounded by the mob Mr Wesley was being dragged along while the rest of the 'army' followed, chanting and yelling. The drummers were beating loudly on their drums all the way in order to incite the 'army' to further acts of violence. Keeping carefully out of sight Tom and his friends followed the crowd. The track ran along beside a river that flowed in a deep gully some ten feet below the surface of the road. The waters were gushing freely; in some places they were deep, while in others rounded boulders broke the surface. They arrived just in time to see the preachers being pushed through the heavy doorway of the *White Bear Inn*. Mr Wesley had demanded that Mr Grimshaw, Thomas Colbeck and one or two others who were with him should also come in but suffer no harm during the hearing.

There was nothing more to do but to wait around for the constable to make his pronouncement. Many who had been listening to Mr Wesley had also followed along the track from Roughlee to Barrowford. Anxious for the welfare of the preachers, they too stayed to hear the outcome of the constable's judgement. Small groups of angry protesters also skulked about the place, impatient for the preachers to appear once more. Clearly further trouble was brewing. While they waited in the hot sun, Tom and his friends, thirsty after their long walk, climbed down the steep bank to the river to scoop a drink of water in their cupped hands. John, the youngest of the gang, lost his balance as he crouched on a slimy green boulder and was soon floundering in the water. Several youths on the bank began to jeer as Tom held out his hand to drag the younger boy back to safety.

Almost an hour later Mr Wesley emerged at last blinking in the bright sunlight, accompanied by the constable. No one knew at that moment on what terms he had gained his release. The restless mob soon saw that they would not be able to assail him further while the constable was protecting him. But where was Mr Grimshaw and the other men with him? Then, with a whoop of triumph, one member of George White's 'army' spotted the curate of Haworth and his young friend Tommy Colbeck, from Keighley, slipping out of a back entrance in the hope of avoiding further trouble. Scarcely had Tom and his gang time to realize what was happening before a wild mob had joined together and was rushing at the two men. Great stones flew through the air. Dirt, sticks, mud, anything to hand, was hurled at them. Again and again Mr Grimshaw deftly dodged the missiles as they came from different directions. Then Tom saw that the curate had been knocked to the ground. He was being mercilessly pelted with dirt and mud, and kicked. Tom and his friends could hardly bear to look — helpless to stop the assault. Then the mob turned on Colbeck and a moment later he too had been thrown on the ground and was being kicked viciously. Grimshaw was soon back on his feet. Above the yells of his attackers came the curate's deep voice, 'Leave 'em to me, Tommy, you with yer spindle-shank legs. I'll show 'em.' And he did. Pushing his way through the throng, he began to fight back against the kickers as only he could. One after another of Colbeck's attackers scattered, each rubbing his bruised shins ruefully. By the end of the tussle Mr Grimshaw's wig was lying in the road, his clerical gown torn and filthy, his usually cheery face plastered with mud. But in that moment Tom Whittaker learnt a new respect for his curate.

Suddenly Tom spotted a familiar-looking figure, one whom he recognized as the leader of a gang of Colne youths. A big loutish fellow with an ugly leer on his face, Alf Sykes had been wielding a cudgel in a dangerous way. If that struck Mr Grimshaw on the head, it could do serious damage. Tom had been waiting for his moment to join the fray. Agile as a cat, he leapt at the youth from behind. Taken completely off-guard, Alf Sykes dropped his cudgel. Big Bob stretched out a long arm and grabbed the offensive weapon and was soon swinging it menacingly around his own head. 'Jest yer wait till I get yer, Tom Whittaker, I'll niver forget this, niver,' snarled the youth helplessly.

Suddenly a stone flew through the air, thrown by another of the Colne gang. It struck Tom on the side of his head. Blood began to flow slowly down his face. At the same moment Mr Grimshaw whirled round. He had heard Tom Whittaker's name. Surely no boy from Haworth could be here? Then he saw Tom and his friends standing nearby. 'Get yerself home at once, Tom Whittaker, and all o' ye, don't yer dare hang around here one bit longer!' he bellowed above the din of the drums and the shouts of the mob. Just at that moment another stone came whirling through the air and only narrowly missed Grimshaw as he quickly ducked. Turning his attention back to his friend from Keighley, who was shaken and hurt by his ordeal, Grimshaw helped Colbeck back to his feet.

Meanwhile the rioters had begun chasing the people who had been listening to Mr Wesley preach and who were still standing nearby. Men, women and even children were thrown to the ground by the mob, kicked, beaten with clubs, and some dragged along the rough path by their hair. One man was ordered to jump down into the river and if he failed to do so, he would be pushed in. He chose to jump; but as he emerged spluttering and gasping from the water and tried to scramble up the bank, Alf Sykes, still intent on harming anyone he could, was waiting at the top and threatening to push him back into the water. Then a second surprise awaited the youth. A moment later he too was up to his neck in the water. Who had pushed him, he never knew, although he had strong suspicions.

Tom and his friends now decided that it would be safer to leave the scene. When Grimshaw turned to see what had happened to the boys, they were nowhere in sight. With Tom's face bleeding badly, they were making for home as fast as they could. Once out of sight of their attackers, and checking that there were no members of the Colne gang lurking around, the boys sat down to rest. John's clothes were slowly drying out, Will seemed unusually quiet and even Big Bob appeared to have had enough. Tom stripped off his shirt and James climbed back down to the river, and soaked a corner of it in the clean clear water. With the wet shirt he dabbed the cut on the side of Tom's head and declared that the wound was 'Nowt t'worry aboot.' The day was cooling down and ahead of them lay a long walk home. All were tired and, to make matters worse, there were still small groups of George White's 'army' hanging around. It would certainly not be safe to take the main road back to Haworth.

Wearily they trudged on, always keeping a keen lookout for anyone hiding around a rock or in the long grasses waiting to spring out on them. After about an hour's walk, John declared that he could go no further and promptly sat down by the side of the track. All of them were hungry, for they had eaten nothing all day apart from the

Site of the Roughlee riot

bread they had brought with them. Will had developed large blisters on his feet. Their pace had become so slow that Tom reckoned that even if John could be persuaded to go further it would be dusk before they reached the Forest of Trawden — not a good place to spend the night.

As he was pondering what to do next Tom noticed the silhouette of a farmhouse against the skyline. He recognized it as Hill Top Farm because only recently his father had sold some pigs to the farmer. The sight of the farmhouse encouraged John to walk a little further, and as the boys approached they saw the farmer's wife outside scattering grain for the chickens. 'Why, if that aint Tom Whittaker!' exclaimed the woman looking up, 'and what d'yer think yer doin' 'ere so far from home?'

Under the scaffold

Kindly the farmer's wife took the boys into the kitchen and gave them chunks of fresh home-made bread and a drink of warm frothy milk. She had the same look on her face as his mother and old Farmer Greenwood; then Tom realized that she too was one of Mr Grimshaw's regular hearers. 'I reckon you lads be too tired to make it home tonight,' she announced. 'How 'bout the night in my barn. There's plenty of soft fresh hay to make you a good bed.' Tom had bad memories of hay barns with his friends, but he was too glad of a place to rest to voice any objections. There would certainly be big trouble awaiting him at home for the anxiety he had caused his parents but he was too tired to worry about it. Before long he and all his friends were fast asleep, breathing in the sweet smell of newly mown hay.

10.
The unforgettable preacher

Two days had passed since the riots at Roughlee. Tom's cut was healing well and he was gradually forgetting the thrashing he had received from his father for causing his mother so much anxiety. News in Haworth always travelled fast and soon Tom discovered that his escapade, together with the other boys in his gang, had become the subject of village gossip. More especially, however, any news concerning their curate William Grimshaw was of great interest in the village. The events at Roughlee and Barrowford were passed excitedly around from one to another, growing ever more dramatic as they were repeated.

Mr Wesley had preached several more times in the area but there had been no further trouble. The next day he was due to return to Bristol where much of his work was centred. As Tom lingered by the Head Well after collecting his water, he learnt some other news that troubled him. Apparently, Mr Wesley had a school down in Bristol — a school mainly for the sons of the miners who had joined the Methodist Societies. Now he had opened a new wing of his school to cater for the children of his preachers. But the thing that concerned Tom was the news that both John and Jane Grimshaw were going to travel with Mr Wesley to Bristol to attend this new school, called the Kingswood School.

Under the scaffold

That John Grimshaw, whose wild behaviour was a further talking point in the village, might well benefit from such a school no one doubted. But what about Jane? Only eleven years of age, she was to be taken far from her moorland home, far from all she had known in her life and far from the father to whom she was devoted. Tom felt sad about it. 'Bristol' — the very name alarmed him. Never had he travelled further than twenty miles from his home, and he was told that Bristol was more than five days journey away. And as if that were not bad enough, it seemed that parents of the Kingswood pupils had to agree neither to visit the school nor to allow their children to come home for at least two years in case they became homesick.

As he was working about the farm the next morning Tom heard the distant sound of horses' hooves ringing on the stony track that led past Old Acre Farm. Looking up he saw the familiar form of Mr Grimshaw on his white horse, and beside him the smaller figure of Mr John Wesley, riding towards him. One or two others who had accompanied Mr Wesley on his journey from the north were riding behind the two men, and next, at the rear of the party, came another horse on which John Grimshaw was riding with his sister clinging on behind him. As the party cantered past Old Acre, Tom looked at Jane. Her face was white and tearful; but as she saw Tom she smiled and waved. And then they were gone. Tom was surprised and ashamed to find a strange lump in his throat. It seemed as if Jane were riding right out of his life altogether. Now he was sure he would never see her again. To a boy of thirteen, two years seemed to stretch far into the distance. An hour afterwards Mr Grimshaw returned alone. Tom could well guess how heavy-hearted he must have felt.

Only a few weeks later Haworth was once again buzzing with excitement. Apparently another famous preacher had just arrived to see their curate. Tom had caught a glimpse of the

The unforgettable preacher

stranger as he rode past Old Acre on his way to Sowdens. A younger man than Mr John, he had a handsome-looking face and the speed with which he cantered past suggested he was an agile horseman. Rumour had it that this preacher had recently returned from the New World where he had spent the last four years, and had preached in many different parts of New England. Tom could not begin to think what it must be like to cross the wild wide ocean in a sailing ship. Apparently the preacher had even established an orphanage at a place called Savannah where many poor children were cared for.

Everywhere this preacher went the crowds followed to hear him preach — vast crowds, so they said, sometimes more than thirty thousand people. Such a figure meant little to Tom. He could hardly imagine what a crowd that size could look like. But he had heard that this new preacher, whose name he had been told was George Whitefield, was going to preach in the Haworth churchyard the following day.

According to the local gossips, on the way home to England from America Mr Whitefield had spent a month on the Bermudas, those strange rocky islands right in the middle of the ocean, which had only been discovered when a ship happened to be wrecked not far from them. The thought of rocky islands with nothing but wild boar and other animals roaming around filled Tom with excitement. How did those shipwrecked mariners ever escape? What did they eat? What did they drink if there was only sea water all around? He was full of questions. Certainly he must go and hear this preacher. Perhaps he would tell some stories of his adventures.

The next evening Tom was astonished to find every road into Haworth choked with men and women, some on horseback, some on foot, some even in horse-drawn carriages. All were pressing up Main Street, along West Lane, Changegate and

Under the scaffold

North Street, and each with one common purpose in mind: to reach St Michael's churchyard. For news had quickly spread throughout the area that George Whitefield would be preaching there that evening and everyone wanted to hear him.

Reaching the churchyard at last, Tom found himself caught up in a teeming mass of bodies and eventually squeezed into a spot not far from the outer wall of the churchyard. He was not tall enough to see the preacher over the heads of the crowd — a crowd that must have numbered almost six thousand people — which were crammed into the wide open space surrounding the church. Just near Tom was a group of soldiers, rough men they seemed, who looked as if they had seen action on many a battlefield. Perhaps they had fought against Bonnie Prince Charlie, Tom thought, as he gazed in admiration at their stained red coats. They were passing crude jokes among themselves, laughing and chatting. Clearly, these men were not really interested in anything Mr Whitefield had to say. Edging away from the soldiers, Tom managed to scale the wall, so gaining a higher position, though a rather precarious one. From this vantage point he could see right across the churchyard. There in the distance he was surprised to catch sight of his friend Will Hartley from the next farm, standing with his mother Jeanie and his eleven-year-old sister Kathy. He found himself hoping that Will had not noticed him. But soon he forgot everything else when he saw the slim outline of the preacher, a man of medium height, climbing on to a large tombstone near the church.

Then he heard it. A voice so clear, so beautiful, so full of melody: like nothing Tom had ever heard before, a sharp contrast to Mr Grimshaw's booming tones. But what was the voice saying? Every word rang out across the churchyard with such clarity and distinctness that the preacher might have been standing only a few yards away. 'Fellow soldiers, fellow soldiers, fellow soldiers,' he was calling in a voice of authority, 'come near!' Could it be true that Mr Whitefield was actually addressing those hardened soldiers standing not far from Tom? It was true. The crowd parted and, unable to do anything except obey, the soldiers slowly made their way to the front of the crowd. Now directing his words to the men standing before

George Whitefield
as Tom would have first seen him.

him as if they were the only ones present, Whitefield addressed them in solemn, urgent tones. He spoke of other rough soldiers, men like themselves, men who had faced death on many battlefields. Those soldiers had flogged the Son of God with cruel whips, they had driven long nails into his hands and feet, had pierced his side with a spear, and had stood mocking the dying Saviour. It was too much: Tom saw those coarse, careless soldiers, who only a few moments before had been laughing and joking, now weeping openly.

And still the preacher went on. 'What! Can you not see your Saviour hanging on a tree with arms stretched out ready to embrace you? Look on his hands, bored with pins of iron; look on his side, pierced with a cruel spear to open a fountain for sin and uncleanness. Can any poor sinner, truly convicted of his sins, despair of mercy after this?' All around him were men and women gripped by every word from the preacher. Tears streamed down many faces, as he began to show that it was not the rough Roman soldiers alone that had crucified Christ, but it was in order to pay for the sins of men, women and young people — even the sins of the people of Haworth — that Christ had endured such anguish.

'Despair of mercy if you can,' continued the voice in those beautifully rounded tones that reminded Tom of the clear bubbling water of the mountain streams that rose on the moors. 'No! only believe in him and then, though you have crucified him afresh, yet will he abundantly pardon you.'[1] Now even the preacher was weeping. Tom could bear it no longer. He was a boy who felt deeply about suffering, both his own and that of others. The thought of the Saviour forgiving those who were hammering cruel nails into his hands was more than he could bear. He must get away from the sound of that voice or he too would be unable to restrain the tears.

He jumped down from the wall and dodged in and out of the crowd as he made his way homeward. But the voice seemed to chase him. Even as he ran along West Lane he could still hear the words, borne on the still evening air. Not until he reached his home did they become a distant blur. He had known before that he was a sinner, but now he knew that his sins had brought unimaginable pain to Jesus Christ.

The next day Mr Whitefield left Haworth to continue his journey up to Scotland, but his words lingered on in Tom's mind for much longer than that. He knew his mother would understand if he spoke to her about it, but a strange shyness gripped the boy. No, this was something he must keep bottled up inside himself.

11.

A passing year

Autumn soon turned to winter once more as biting winds swept down from the moors, howling round Old Acre Farm, while freezing temperatures numbed Tom's fingers and toes. Winter days seemed endless, but gradually, as 1749 dawned, the ice on ponds and streams began to thaw and before long the busy lambing season had begun. Not many days before he died Farmer Greenwood had bequeathed his flock of sheep and goats to Tom. With no relatives of his own, he had loved the boy like a son. So now, with double the number of animals to care for, Tom and his father worked early and late helping with difficult births, and nurturing orphaned or rejected lambs. The family vegetable plot too needed planting up with cabbages, carrots and onions.

Before long all nature seemed bursting with new and exuberant life. Up on the moors the clouds chased each other across the sky, new bracken unfurled its soft green fronds and the birds sang as though they had all entered a singer-of-the-year competition. Tom himself had put the thoughts that had perplexed him after he had heard George Whitefield preach to the back of his mind, although now and then after he had listened to one of Mr Grimshaw's sermons they returned to challenge him.

Under the scaffold

Tom's younger brother George had turned ten and an unspoken truce had grown up between the brothers — in fact Tom had now become George's hero. The younger boy was growing ever more useful on the farm; and had even been known to offer to fetch the water when Tom was too busy to do it. Margaret, at seventeen, had gone into service to help out with the family finances. She had gained a coveted place at the Old Hall, home of the Emmott family, which stood at the foot of Main Street. Here she washed the laundry, cleaned, and stoked up the fires for the household. Just opposite the Old Hall lay the Ducking Pond, and Margaret had Tom and George in fits of laughter as she described the day she saw sharp-tongued Mrs Tavers being tied to a stool attached to a long plank, and then, despite loud protests, being solemnly dipped three times into the slimy stagnant water to cure her of scolding her neighbours and nagging poor Pete Tavers. Molly remained the family favourite and at seven years of age, with her fair hair and bright eyes, reminded Tom of Alice, the sister he had lost at just that age.

Tom himself was fast growing up. At fourteen he was tall and strong. He had even begun to try to tame his unruly thatch of hair. He must endeavour to impress the village girls and particularly Patsy Walters from nearby Stanhope, who, with her mother, always sat not far from the Whittaker family on a Sunday. Twice, Tom noted, she had turned round and given him a quick smile when Mr Grimshaw was not looking. But despite Tom's best efforts stray tufts of hair still seemed to protrude at odd angles. 'I love you as you are,' Mary had told her older son, but her remark had only embarrassed Tom and made little difference to his efforts.

Of Tom's group of friends, Will Hartley from the next farm, James Clayton and even John Dene, who was still only twelve, had been sent off to nearby villages to undertake apprenticeships.

A passing year

Only Big Bob Bradshaw remained in the village and, like his father Jake, was becoming a skilled blacksmith. A hefty fellow, Bob tended to be a bully at times and sometimes joined the older youths in harassing members of the community who attended the evening prayer meetings held in different homes in Haworth and the surrounding villages. But Bob was no leader and would rarely initiate or even take a prominent part in the nightly 'raids' the youths would make. Instead he hung back enjoying the fun of seeing the fear written on the faces of the elderly villagers.

But one afternoon as Tom was finishing cleaning out the pigsties, a task he did not enjoy, Big Bob arrived at Old Acre with a story to tell that set both the boys laughing until the tears rolled down their cheeks. Apparently, the previous night as the gang had approached a cottage in a place about a mile from Haworth known as The Marsh, they had begun as usual to push and jostle the folk who were arriving and entering the cottage. But every now and then an old woman inside the cottage, wearing a frilly lace cap, poked her head around the door and had a quick look around. Perhaps she was checking up that she had no more visitors before closing the door and beginning the prayer meeting.

Out popped the quaint-looking lace-capped head again — and yet again. The temptation was too great. The youths began to taunt and jibe, and advance ever nearer. And still the strange-looking woman thrust her head out for a brief moment, peered around and then disappeared. 'If that old woman puts her head out of that door once more,' exclaimed Paul Beaver, leader of the youths, 'I will seize her!' Out came the head, and Paul Beaver lunged forward to give the old thing a blow in the face that would prevent her from putting out her head again for a very long time. In a flash the young man felt his wrists held in an iron grip so powerful, so unyielding, that struggle as he might, he could not escape. Dragged into the cottage, Paul Beaver found that the lace-capped head belonged to none other than William Grimshaw himself. Once again he had used disguise to detect troublemakers in his parish. Bewildered and astonished, Beaver was forced to confess the names of those who had been with him, and each youth was ordered to appear before the curate in the church the following day. The 'old woman' had not noticed Big Bob lurking in the shadows, nor did Beaver consider him as part of his gang, but that night Tom's friend made a solemn decision: never again would he mock or molest people attending a prayer meeting.

Since his friendship with the Methodist leaders, John and Charles Wesley and George Whitefield, William Grimshaw had been ever bolder in preaching in the outlying districts around Haworth, and sometimes much further afield. Rochdale, Manchester, Bacup and even Chester and Sheffield had visits from the curate of Haworth. Sometimes he faced angry and unruly mobs, stirred up by resentful local clergy, but nothing seemed to deter him from his mission to preach the message of forgiveness of sin wherever he could. Often on a Monday morning after three or even four services in Haworth, Grimshaw would canter past Old Acre Farm on his faithful white horse, bound for some distant location. Tom would watch him go, wondering where he was off to. With John and Jane away in Bristol, he no longer had any family commitments to keep him in Haworth, and could sometimes be away for two or three days at a time. Yet in spite of this he seemed to know all that was going on in the village, and if ever a family was in trouble or had any special concerns, the curate's heavy tread would soon be heard approaching the home.

News of Jane and John Grimshaw was scarce. But the scraps of information that did filter through to the villagers were not reassuring. Rules were strict at the New House, as the recently-opened wing of Kingswood School was called. Girls, in particular, were to be kept occupied from early in the morning until they crept thankfully into their beds at eight o'clock at night. 'She who plays when she is a child will play when she is a woman' was the principle that Mr Wesley had laid down. Pupils were expected to spend each Friday in fasting and prayer if they were in good health. Although John and Jane were receiving an excellent education compared with the standard they would have received had they remained in Haworth, Jane had not settled well. She missed her father's warm affection and the sound of his hearty voice; she missed the wide open spaces of the moorland where she could wander at will; she even missed seeing Tom Whittaker whom she had considered as a sort of hero, ever since he had rescued her when she trapped her foot on the moors. Concerned about his children, her father had actually travelled down to Bristol on one occasion, against the advice of Mr Wesley, and had discovered that both John and Jane had lost a great deal of weight and Jane in particular seemed far from well. But because he had agreed that he would not bring them home during the course of their education, he had felt bound to honour his word.

The summer months of 1749 passed quickly for Tom and his family. But in the early autumn of that year an outbreak of smallpox in the village left behind it many sorrowful homes as it seemed to strike at random at both young and old. Mary watched her children, anxiously looking for early symptoms of the dreaded killer-disease. But when she and Jack heard that their neighbours' younger son Dick had been taken ill, they were deeply troubled, firstly for Robert and Jeanie Hartley's sake and then for their own, for seven-year-old Dick would often come to Old Acre to play with Molly. But worse was to follow. Although

Under the scaffold

Dick Hartley made a gradual recovery, his mother Jeanie, who had been nursing him night and day, succumbed to the infection and died.

The loss of her childhood friend was a severe blow for Mary Whittaker. The two women had enjoyed an uncommon friendship, particularly in recent years when Jeanie too had responded to the preaching of their curate William Grimshaw and found forgiveness for her sins. Tom's friend Will came home for the funeral and for his sake Tom also attended the service although it brought back a flood of memories of both Alice and Farmer Greenwood. The unspoken question in everyone's mind was how thirteen-year-old Kathy — Jeanie and Robert's older daughter — would cope with caring for her father, her younger sister, nine-year-old Annie, and her brother Dick. She would certainly not find it easy and Mary Whittaker determined that for the sake of her friend Jeanie she would do all she could to help Kathy.

Gradually the epidemic of smallpox died out and village life returned to normal. Towards the end of September Tom heard that George Whitefield was expected back in Haworth once more. A year had passed since Tom had heard the preacher and now he found himself with mixed feelings. Torn between a wish to hear him preach and a fear of the effect that might have upon him, he scarcely knew what to do. When Mr Whitefield rode up Main Street and along West Lane the people greeted him joyfully. He had to pass Old Acre Farm on his way to Sowdens and just at that moment Tom happened to be coming along the track with Tivvy, the collie, after checking up on the condition of the sheep. The preacher stopped, dismounted and spoke kindly to the boy, asking him his name and where he lived, before continuing on his way. Tom was most impressed. How could someone who could hold thirty thousand people spellbound by his words take an interest in a poor farmer's son? He noticed a strange squint in one of the preacher's eyes, but somehow it did not spoil his appearance — in fact it even added interest to his handsome features.

That Sunday Jack Whittaker announced that he would be going to the Sunday market in Bradford to sell his wools and to buy in more raw materials. Tom must accompany him as he needed his help. Glad of an excuse for not listening to the preacher whose earlier message had moved him so strangely, Tom gladly agreed, and George was understandably jealous of his older brother. By the time Jack and Tom arrived home, night was falling across the village. All along the road on the way back they had met with streams of men and women who had crowded to Haworth to hear the preacher. As the people returned to their homes, all seemed aglow with joy at the messages they had heard, for George Whitefield had preached three times that day, once again to congregations numbering up to six thousand people.

Soon winter days returned, cutting off the village from all around. Heavy snow lay like a blanket over the moors and mists hung low, blotting out all but the immediate surroundings from view. The weather did not appear to deter Mr Grimshaw from his mission. Buttoned up in a heavy jacket, he plodded through the snow, either to reach a sick parishioner far out on the moors or to preach in some distant village where he was expected. Tom shuddered as he saw him pass the house and wondered how it was that he could carry on his work with such diligence regardless of the freezing temperatures.

One day, late in January 1750, a messenger toiled up Main Street bringing a letter for Mr Grimshaw — a letter written in neat handwriting — from his son John. The curate had a visitor staying at Sowdens when the letter was delivered and this friend recorded in his diary the contents of that letter. John was breaking the sad news to his father that on 14 January his sister Jane had died in Bristol. Jane had been unhappy at being so far from her home and her longing for the comfort of her father's presence had grown ever more acute. With lowered resistance she had succumbed to one of those winter epidemics that so often swept through communities. But during her illness, as John told his father, Jane had found comfort in the Lord Jesus Christ. 'For some time before she was taken ill my sister became very pensive and thoughtful. "Something wonderful is going to happen here," she told me.' Although she had been ill for some weeks, Jane had 'borne up wonderfully'. One morning when the child was very low the teacher went into her room. She heard the twelve-year-old speaking quietly to herself and thought she must be praying. Then quite suddenly in a clear strong voice Jane had called out some words from a hymn written by Charles Wesley:

> He has loved me, I cried,
> he has suffered and died
> to redeem such a rebel as me.

That was all. And then Jane was gone; gone to a better home prepared for her in heaven — a home which she would never have to leave.

It was a devastating blow for her father. As his visitor recorded, 'Jane was very near and dear to him.' Perhaps he wondered why he had let her go to Bristol. But what else could he do? With his wife dead, the grandparents increasingly frail, his own work taking him away from his home so often, who was there to look after Jane? Without delay Grimshaw prepared for the long journey down to Bristol, made even more difficult by the severe winter conditions. But Jane had already been buried for well over a fortnight by the time he arrived in early February. His friend Charles Wesley, who lived in Bristol together with his wife Sally, welcomed the bereaved father into his home — and was able to comfort him in his loss.

John Grimshaw too was glad to see his father. He also was looking gaunt and thin, and without a second thought his father decided to take John home with him when he returned to Haworth a few days later. At fourteen, and not particularly given to studying, John would be better if he were apprenticed to some trade, his father decided.

Tom reacted strangely to the news of Jane's death. It stunned and challenged him but never did he pass a single comment on the event — surprising for a boy who usually had plenty to say about everything. He had been very fond of Jane in an odd sort of way. She had been the same age as Alice and similar in many respects; and as he looked at her he would imagine what Alice might have been like if she had lived. He had felt a degree of tenderness towards her ever since he had rescued her on the moors. But now Jane too had died. And from what her brother John had said about her, she was ready for death. Tom knew only too well that he was not. At nearly fifteen years of age, he had already experienced the loss of three people he cared about, in addition to his infant sister. Surely he must begin to face the issues this raised. But Tom Whittaker was not yet ready for that. He thrust such thoughts to the back of his mind.

12.
The old woman on the moors

In the summer of 1750 and again in October 1752 George Whitefield was back in Haworth once more. A warm friendship had been built up between the robust village curate and the highly-sought-after preacher. It seemed as if he could not stay away. Describing this 1752 visit, Whitefield had written to a friend, 'I have scarcely known whether I have been in heaven or on earth.' Then he added, 'Thousands and thousands have flocked twice or three times a day to hear the word of life.' So great was the eagerness of the people of Haworth and the outlying districts to hear the preacher that some climbed up on to nearby rooftops and others even scaled the tower of the church, clinging on precariously in case they fell. But Tom Whittaker was not among those 'thousands and thousands' who crowded to hear George Whitefield preach. In fact he found excuses to prevent him from being there. It was not that Tom was unconcerned about the message that both Mr Grimshaw and Mr Whitefield preached. Far from it. The reverse was true. He was so troubled by the issues that the preaching raised in his mind that he hardly dared to think about them.

Tom was now seventeen years of age. Medium in height and good-looking, he was as talkative as ever and with the same mischievous streak in his personality. He was proving invaluable to his father on the farm, and particularly now that Jack Whittaker had added a small herd of milking cows to his stock. George, too, at thirteen had become most useful, but Jack had decided that his younger son should take up the apprenticeship as a wheelwright that he had considered for Tom — a skill which would always earn the boy a living even if the farm should fail. So George was now in nearby Heptonstall, and even though the brothers had become good friends, they were seldom able to meet. Molly was a little spoilt, but at the age of ten was beginning to help her mother in the combing and spinning of the wools that formed so important a part of the family income.

Mary Whittaker had remembered her resolve to help her friend Jeanie Hartley's daughter Kathy whenever she could, but life in Haworth was a long round of toil and few opportunities seemed to present themselves. However, when the girl's father injured his arm just as the hay needed scything and storing up for winter, Mary asked Tom if he could help out. Strong and skilled, Tom soon had the field cleared with the help of ten-year-old Dick Hartley. Kathy, who was now sixteen, arrived on the scene with some of her home-made bread and a drink — a gesture that Tom, hungry as ever, was not slow to appreciate.

From early morning until darkness fell, Tom and his father were normally kept busy on their own farm. And even after dark there were often tasks that had to be done. Animals still needed feeding and tending, and of course the daily milking of the cows took much time. Even Molly was becoming quite an expert little milkmaid. But Sunday was different. Under the careful teaching and watchful eye of William Grimshaw the day had become one when all work, except for unavoidable duties, came to an abrupt end.

Tom's friend Big Bob had told him of the day when a distraught young man had hammered on his father's door early one Sunday morning. The man's wife was about to give birth to a child and he had been riding across the moors in great haste to fetch the midwife. But his horse had suddenly lost a shoe and he could go no further. Whatever could he do? Surely Bob's father, Jake Bradshaw, the blacksmith, would help him, and open up his forge even though it was a Sunday. 'Nay, mon, that I canna,' replied the honest blacksmith. Panic-stricken, the father-to-be pleaded with Big Bob's father. At last he conceded that they would go together to Sowdens and obtain permission from the curate for such a work of mercy — a request that William Grimshaw did not hesitate to grant. And before long the man was riding off into the distance with the midwife bumping along behind him.

The young people of Haworth, however, had other ideas about how to spend their Sundays. With the girls freed from their daily round of combing and spinning and weaving the wool, of cleaning and cooking, of caring for the younger children, nothing gave them greater pleasure than to join up with the lads on the moors on a Sunday evening. The hidden dells and disused quarries dotted across the moors were ideal meeting places, and at first their activities consisted of no more than innocent games and general chatter. But gradually their 'fun' became increasingly questionable.

Tom regularly slipped off to the moors on a Sunday night after the evening milking was finished. He was surprised that Kathy Hartley from Meadow Head Farm never seemed to want to join the group even though she had often been invited. Perhaps the responsibilities of caring for her younger brother and sister meant that she had no time, he thought. On the other hand, he knew she attended St Michael's regularly, and wondered if she disapproved of their activities. But it was of little consequence to Tom in any case because Patsy Walters from Stanhope had now become a close friend. With her round cheerful face and laughing eyes, the plump sixteen-year-old fascinated Tom. Somehow, when he was with her, the serious thoughts that so often troubled him, particularly at nights — thoughts of his sins, of the life to come and even of Farmer Greenwood's last wish that they might meet again one day — seemed far off, even foolish.

At first William Grimshaw had said little about the young people's Sunday evening get-togethers. But gradually matters began to grow more serious. Rumours started to spread among the villagers of far more dubious behaviour up on the moors. And when Maggi Peters from Spring Head Farm was forced to confess that she was pregnant, Grimshaw began to denounce their behaviour from the pulpit in the most stringent words: 'What!' he exclaimed, 'do you think you can dance with the devil all day and then sup with Christ at night? Shame it is to live so short a time in the world and do so much evil. The flower of life is of Christ's setting, and shall it be for the devil's plucking? Will you hang the most sparkling jewel of your young years in the devil's ears?' Then came words that made Tom shudder when someone told him of them: 'If God's day seems too soon for *your* repentance, *your* to-morrow may be too late for *him* to accept you.' That was indeed frightening. What if he had put off all his opportunities to turn from his sins, and now it was too late?

Just in case Mr Grimshaw should decide to come strolling across the moors to try to discover which of the young people met in this way on a Sunday night, the choice of meeting place was rearranged from week to week, and here Tom's excellent knowledge of the moors came into its own. But even so, Hoyle Syke Green proved the most popular location. There was plenty of shelter so that they could hide quickly if the curate should be spotted in the distance and a nearby prominence where the lookout could see for a long way across the moor. Jack turned a blind eye to his son's behaviour. As long as Tom worked hard all day on the farm, he was not too troubled about what the boy got up to on a Sunday evening. With Mary it was different. Often she spoke to Tom, warning him that Patsy was not a good friend for him and urging him not to join the young people on the moors. Sometimes when he came home late at night he thought his mother had been crying, but he was not quite sure, and anyway, what business was it of hers what he did or did not do up on the moors?

Weeks passed and still the young people met secretly on Sunday nights. Travellers sometimes crossed the moors and it was the task of the one on lookout duty to check the identity if possible of the person or people approaching. Mostly it was worshippers making their way homeward in small groups after a Sunday in Haworth.

One night it was Patsy Walters' turn to stand as lookout and to warn the others of any approaching danger. One or two groups of people had drifted past, but no one to worry about. Dark clouds were now beginning to gather as night drew in, and Patsy was feeling cold. But still she remained on duty. At last the group decided on one last dance before they separated. They had all linked hands and were standing in a large circle. Just then Patsy noticed an old woman approaching. Bent and grey, with a large shawl over her shoulders, she seemed to be finding the going difficult. Every now and then she stopped and appeared to stumble. As she came near the place where Patsy was standing she did a strange thing. She took out a piece of paper from under her shawl and began to write something down. As most old women could neither read nor write, this was very suspicious. Then instead of passing by the group of young people and continuing on her way, she approached the circle, broke into it and linked hands with two of the young people as if she wanted to join in the dance. How odd!

Tom was standing opposite the old woman. He was looking at her legs. What strange legs for such a person. And they looked familiar too. Where had he seen those legs before? Then in a flash he knew. They were Mr Grimshaw's sturdy legs. Daring to raise his eyes a little higher, he looked straight into the face of the curate. 'Run for it!' he hissed. In panic the whole circle dropped hands and fled. The only two who remained were the unfortunate two on either side of Mr Grimshaw. Their hands were locked fast in his iron grip. 'I know who you are,' he announced calmly, 'and I know the names of most of the young people who have been here tonight. I want you all to attend at the vestry without fail tomorrow evening at six o'clock.'

The hours of Monday dragged slowly past. What would Mr Grimshaw say? Tom had heard that he had actually taken a horsewhip to a group of young thugs who were pushing and even injuring villagers who had been trying to attend a prayer meeting. Would they receive the same treatment? But in one way Tom did not fear that as much as the thought that he had disgraced himself in the eyes of the curate; for deep down he respected, even admired, him. Shamed-faced and apprehensive, Tom made his way slowly towards the vestry that evening. It was no good trying to persuade himself that Mr Grimshaw had not seen him. He knew he had.

Most of the others were already there when Tom arrived, including Patsy Walters and Big Bob. Mr Grimshaw was waiting for them. As they shuffled into the vestry one by one, Tom thought he caught just the trace of a twinkle in his curate's eye. Perhaps he knew what it was like to be young after all. But any thought that Mr Grimshaw was not serious about the conduct of the young people on the moors soon vanished. When they were all seated he delivered a scorching lecture on the sins of immorality. His words flowed relentlessly on and soon Patsy started sobbing and so did two or three of the other girls. As Tom listened he began to tremble almost without being able to help himself. It was as if hell was opening up its mouth and was just ready to swallow him up.

However, the next moment the curate did an extraordinary thing. He fell on his knees in the middle of the circle of young offenders and began to pour out his heart in prayer for them. One by one he mentioned their names before the throne of God: their circumstances, their needs, their sins, and pleaded with God to show his mercy towards them for the sake of his Son, Jesus Christ. Just a moment ago it had seemed to Tom that hell was about to eat him up, now heaven appeared open before him, and Jesus Christ was standing there at God's right hand, ready to forgive his sins. There might yet be hope for him. As the group filed sheepishly out of the vestry, Tom for one decided that he would not be found up on the moors again on a Sunday evening and, in fact, that particular gathering was never resumed.

13.
The revenge

Three years had slipped past since that night when William Grimshaw had discovered the whereabouts of the young people on the moors — years that had seen a number of changes in the Whittakers' family life. It was now 1755 and Margaret, Tom's older sister, was in her early twenties. An efficient young woman, she had married Paul Beaver, the youth who had tried to strike the old 'woman' wearing a lace cap at the cottage prayer meeting. Paul had been deeply impressed by some words from the curate shortly after that event and although he had made no profession of faith had become a diligent, conscientious man. He and Margaret were looking forward to the birth of their first child.

Tom, who was now a fine-looking young man of twenty, was gradually taking over more responsibility for the farm from his father. George, at nearly seventeen, had almost completed his apprenticeship as a wheelwright, but was anxious to return to the farm, where he hoped to combine his newly-acquired skills with his duties there. Thirteen-year-old Molly had taken Margaret's place as her mother's assistant in the cottage. An intelligent girl, her quick nimble fingers proved an invaluable help to Mary in the combing and spinning of the wools. Molly was a great favourite with Tom and whenever he could he included his attractive young sister as he went about his duties on the farm. Mary herself, now in her fifties, was finding the work ever more tiring and was grateful for her young daughter's help.

Things were changing in Haworth as well. At last in June 1755 the long-needed enlargement of the church had begun. Huge congregations had continued to pour into the village each Sunday, and when either of the Wesley brothers or George Whitefield was in the area, the numbers wishing to attend the services had become nearly impossible to accommodate, even in the expansive churchyard. It had taken ten years to raise the necessary funds for the alterations to the church building for most of the people of Haworth were poor, finding it hard enough to feed their own families adequately. The new church would be almost square in shape, seating more than five hundred. In addition the walls were to be raised in order to accommodate galleries around three of the four sides, although the tower would remain untouched. The most significant change, however, was the removal of Mr Grimshaw's large three-tiered pulpit to the south side of the church, next to one of the windows, so that the preacher could climb out of the window with ease and stand on a large wooden scaffold-like platform which would be erected in the churchyard. From there he could address the thousands who stood outside and also be heard by those within the church.

Tom watched all these changes with a mixture of curiosity and astonishment, but he was not attending the services of the church at all now. The memory of Jane Grimshaw and even of Farmer Greenwood was fading. He avoided meeting Mr Grimshaw whenever he could, and if he heard his horse coming along the lane, Tom would always find some task to which he must attend that would take him to the back of the farm. But this did not mean that Tom was not often troubled in his mind about his neglect of spiritual issues. The sight of two different people kept reminding him that all was not right with him. The first was his mother. She said little to Tom, but he was aware that she spent much time praying for him. He hated to distress her and decided that if George came back to the farm, he himself would rent a smallholding of his own. Then he would no longer have to face his mother's worried looks.

The second was Kathy Hartley from the next farm. Kathy was now nineteen and had become a beautiful young woman with long dark hair and brown expressive eyes. Her life had not been easy since her mother had died in the smallpox epidemic of 1749. Impractical and dreamy by nature, she had found it hard to run the home until her younger sister Annie had been old enough to help out. However, things were easier for Kathy now, even though Annie had left home to take up the place at Emmott Hall which Tom's sister Margaret had held before she married. Kathy's older brother Will, who had been Tom's friend, had been apprenticed to the shoe trade and now worked in Halifax, but Dick helped his father on the farm. The responsibilities Kathy had shouldered in the last six years had made it hard for her to cultivate any friendships outside of her home and although Tom had long admired Kathy, he sometimes felt that he scarcely knew her, even though they had lived at neighbouring farms all their lives.

Tom's friendship with Patsy Walters had come to an unhappy end several years earlier, particularly when it became clear to Tom that Patsy was wanting more from him than he was prepared to give. Added to this, she was proving an easy catch for the young men of the village, courting their attentions while at the same time trying to deceive Tom into thinking that this was not the case. Before long Patsy's immoral lifestyle brought untold shame upon both herself and her parents as she became pregnant and was at a loss to name which young man was the father of her child. William Grimshaw openly rebuked the girl for her behaviour, warning all the young people of Haworth of the fearful end of such conduct without due repentance.

But Kathy Hartley was not like that and Tom knew it. Not long after her mother's death she had responded personally to the message Mr Whitefield preached and even Tom could see that she now seemed to have an inner strength, enabling her to cope with her circumstances. Although Kathy had frequently been invited to join the group who used to meet up on the moors each Sunday night, and had often felt tempted to do so, she had resisted the pressure although it had meant that she was even more cut off from the other young people of Haworth. It had not been easy, and now at nineteen, when many young women had established homes of their own, Kathy was still unmarried. The longing for friendship and understanding had sometimes become so intense that she scarcely knew how to contain it. Not that she had lacked opportunities to form relationships with the young men of the village. In recent months a number had made pressing and often suggestive proposals to her; it was only her desire to please God that had given her an inner resolve to reject such overtures. Although Tom was attracted to Kathy, he had not made any advances to the girl because he was well aware that he could never hope to gain her affection with his present attitudes to those things that clearly mattered to her. Nor was he prepared to make any religious profession just to impress her.

The most surprising thing of all in the Whittaker family at the time was the unaccountable behaviour of Jack Whittaker himself. Even though the taverns were officially closed on a Sunday, for years Jack had always disappeared on a Sunday morning, creeping in to the *Black Bull* by some back entrance and enjoying a lazy pint or two of ale with the other farmers. Although William Grimshaw or one of the church wardens would often perform a random check on the three drinking houses that ringed the church, Jack had managed to avoid detection. And he still disappeared each Sunday morning. Mary had long ceased urging him to attend the services with her, and always tried instead to cover up for her husband's weaknesses. The strange thing was, and it was Tom who first noticed it, that although Jack was still cheerful enough when he returned, his breath no longer smelt of alcohol. And other things were different too. He was slower to fly into a rage when things went wrong on the farm, and seemed kinder in his disposition towards Mary. Tom spoke to his mother about it, but even she seemed a little bemused. So he decided to investigate himself.

'Have yer seen my Pa on a Sunday morning recently?' Tom enquired of several of Jack's fellow drinkers.

'Why, no, m'lad,' was the reply from one and another. 'He aint bin here for some weeks.' Then Tom guessed. His father must be listening to Mr Grimshaw preaching on a Sunday morning. With hundreds crowding every corner of the churchyard and the seating within the church itself disrupted owing to the rebuilding work, it was easy enough for one man to attend without anyone else knowing of it. That explained everything.

One bright morning in August of that year Jack announced that he wished to take some sides of bacon and other produce for sale in the Colne market. 'It'll take us a couple of hours to get there, Tom, so could yer get Floss harnessed up while I load the cart?' Before long Tom and his father were jogging along the road at a smart rate. Floss was an excitable young mare that Jack had recently bought in place of Belle who had served the family for as long as Tom could remember, and who now spent her days grazing in the meadow behind the farm. Tom had become an expert young horseman and Jack was contented to let his son take the reins.

By five o'clock in the afternoon, with their business in Colne almost complete, Tom was harnessing Floss once more in readiness for their homeward journey. Just at that moment he caught a glimpse of a face he half recognized. It was only a brief glimpse and then the face disappeared. For a moment Tom could not think who it was: a spotty lopsided face with an ugly leer. Then he remembered. Of course, it was Alf Sykes, the leader of the Colne gang, the youth who had been wielding a cudgel at the Roughlee riots seven years ago. Alf was taller now, but from his looks it would appear that his nature was unchanged. Tom shuddered as he remembered that day.

Floss seemed as anxious to reach the farm as Jack and Tom, and soon the small cart was bowling along at a speedy rate. It had been a successful day. Jack had sold all his produce and obtained a satisfactory price for the sides of bacon. The money would come in useful with the monthly rent almost due. Tom was driving and whistling cheerfully to himself; Jack was feeling a little sleepy and was sitting in the empty cart, his legs dangling out the back. They were not more than a mile out of Colne when they came to a sharp bend in the road. 'Whoa there!' cried Tom with a light flick of his whip. Floss must take the bend slowly or the small cart could overturn.

Just as they rounded the corner Tom caught another sickening glimpse of that face. Leaping up from behind a rock was none other than Alf Sykes. He was holding a large stone in his hand. 'I allus sed I'd get evens wi' yer, Tom Whittaker,' he yelled. 'Jest yer take that!' And the next moment the stone was hurtling through the air towards Tom. Tom ducked sharply, but in fact there was no need. Alf's aim was poor, and instead of hitting Tom the stone struck Floss sharply on the rump. With a wild neigh of pain the young mare reared high in the air, and the next moment the small cart was pitched onto its side, throwing both Tom and Jack out on the road. 'Ha! Ha! Ha!' called a voice as Alf Sykes disappeared into the distance, back towards Colne. Ruefully Tom picked himself up. His shin and elbow were bleeding, but otherwise, although badly shaken, he was unhurt.

Floss had dragged the upturned cart a few yards further on and had then come to a standstill. But what about Jack? Tom ran quickly to where his father lay, face down. 'Pa! Pa! are yer hurt?' he cried. Jack did not answer. Then Tom saw that his father had hit his head against a boulder as he had fallen and was unconscious. Whatever was he going to do? Jack was a big man and Tom could not move him on his own; also he knew it would be unsafe to try to lift him by himself. But he could not imagine anyone else coming along that lonely track at this time of day. Walking over to the cart he spoke gently to Floss and examined the cut on her back. It was not serious and, when the mare was calm enough, Tom managed to turn the small cart upright once more. Then he returned and sat down beside his father. A low groan reassured him that Jack was still alive.

How long Tom sat there, he did not know. He dared not leave Jack and return to Colne for help. Who could tell whether Alf Sykes and his gang might be back? If only someone would come. The sun was setting behind the nearby hill and before long night would close in. Tom's mind flashed back to that time when he had sat by his mother after the birth of the baby. God had heard his prayer then, but how could he expect God to hear him now? Tom had neglected God, it seemed only right that God should neglect him.

Just as darkness was beginning to shroud the scene, Tom thought he could hear far off the sound of a horse's hooves.

Perhaps he was mistaken. He listened again. No, it was definitely a horse's hooves and the sound was growing louder. Perhaps it was Alf Sykes returning to torment him. Defensively Tom rose to his feet, ready to use his fists if necessary should anyone attempt to touch Jack. He walked to the bend in the road to see if he could see who might be coming. Then a familiar figure rode into sight. Tom could have wept with relief. It was none other than Mr Grimshaw, returning late from some preaching service.

Dismounting quickly, the curate came to where Jack was lying, and bent down for a few moments over him. Slowly he rose; his face looked grave. 'I think we will be able to lift him between us, Tom,' he said after a while. 'You go and fetch the cart and then we will try.' Before they attempted to lift Jack, Mr Grimshaw insisted that they should pray for God's help. Tom bowed his head silently as the curate prayed. Surely God would hear that prayer, thought Tom, even though he could not expect his own prayers to be heard.

Slowly, gently, they managed to lift the injured man and to lay him down in the cart; then Tom returned to the driving seat. Grimshaw rode slowly beside them all the way back to Old Acre Farm. Standing at the gate of the farm was Mary, clutching Molly's hand, anxiety written all over her face. As the hours had crept past she realized beyond doubt that either her husband or her son must be in serious trouble. Grimshaw spoke briefly to Mary and then helped Tom to carry his father into the house. By this time Jack had regained consciousness, but was clearly badly hurt. The curate stayed with the distressed family until late into the night. He had been preaching in Roughlee once more, he told Tom. George White, the curate of Colne, had died two years earlier — a poor broken man — with his life ruined by alcohol. But as he was dying he had asked William Grimshaw to come and speak to him and had begged his forgiveness for the events that day at Roughlee. 'I hope and pray that all was well with his soul, Tom,' Grimshaw had added.

For the next three days the family gathered around the couch on which Jack had been laid. He had suffered serious head injuries when he struck the boulder as he fell. His daughter Margaret called in each day to see him and George returned from Heptonstall. Mary's distress was obvious to all the family, and only when Tom insisted that she must snatch a few hours of sleep would she leave Jack's side. Yet Jack himself looked strangely peaceful. For most of the time he was conscious, but he spoke little. Whenever Mr Grimshaw called, as he did each day on his way to inspect the progress of the building of the church, Jack's face lit up. Mr Grimshaw would read to him from the Bible, beautiful passages that Tom did not know were in there. One especially struck Tom: it was about a thief who was apparently dying at the same time as Jesus, and Jesus had said, 'Today you will be with me in paradise.' That must have been very wonderful, thought Tom. Then Mr Grimshaw would pray with Jack, but Tom always left the room at that point.

Jack's periods of unconsciousness were growing more frequent. Of all the family, it was probably Tom who was the most distressed. His father had been his friend and companion ever since the boy was able to undertake small jobs on the farm. Tom now knew beyond a doubt that his father was dying. But most bitter of all for Tom was the fact that he felt himself to blame for Jack's injury. If he had not gone to Roughlee that day and leapt up on Alf Sykes this would never have happened, he told himself over and over again.

Tom was sitting beside his father on the fourth day after the accident, his head buried in his hands. Thinking Jack was unconscious, Tom began to moan aloud. 'Oh Pa! Pa! it's all my fault. Yer sufferin' for what I done. I'm scared you'll die and I'm t' blame. Oh, I'm t' blame, Pa. It's all my fault, my fault, and I can never forgive myself.'

Quite suddenly Jack opened his eyes. He had not been unconscious at all. 'Tom, Tom, m'lad, don't yer carry on like that, tha maun do it.' Tom started and looked steadily at his father. The glazed look had gone and he was speaking slowly and clearly. 'And, Tom, there's another thing. Yer see, Someone else suffered for all t' bad things I ever done in m' life. Jesus has forgiven me, Tom, and tha must forgive Alf Sykes. I'm jest like that there thief as Mr Grimshaw read about. Now I'm goin' t' his paradise, but, Tom, I've left it too late t' do awt for him in return. Don't yer leave it too late m'boy...' his voice was trailing off now... 'P'haps one day yer can serve him instead o' me...' That was all. Jack's eyes had closed once more. In fact he never spoke again.

14.
Kathy

News of the incident and of Jack Whittaker's subsequent death travelled quickly throughout the area. Jack had been a popular figure in the community and people came from far and wide to attend his funeral. William Grimshaw had a special word of comfort for Mary. 'If a man and his wife are invited to dine with a friend, and he sets out an hour before her, would their parting be bitter if both are to dine together at noon?' he had asked. 'And if Jack has set out for heaven a short while before you, you must not grieve. You will be together again ere long.' Mary smiled through her tears at the thought of her Jack, who was always hungry, sitting down at some heavenly feast hardly able to wait until she had arrived.

But Tom was not smiling. Nor was he crying. His father's death had hit him hard, and particularly the circumstances surrounding it. Almost the last thing Jack had said to Tom was that he must forgive Alf Sykes. But that he could not and would not do. Anger burned in his heart against the bully whose wicked action had robbed him of his father, and robbed his mother of the one on whom she had so completely depended. Before long that anger turned to hatred: fierce, dark hatred. Night after night he turned over schemes of vengeance, even of murder, planning what he could do to take that leer off Alf Sykes' face for ever. He saw that face in his dreams — and always it was chasing him, destroying him.

Had Tom known it, Alf Sykes was already suffering a severe punishment for his action. Never popular before, he was now despised and shunned by the whole community. Small children ran away as soon as they saw him coming, warned by their mothers, and from a distance would chant their taunts, reminding him of what he had done. He had held a job as an assistant in the local smithy. Now his employer told him that his services were no longer required. His mother was a widow and even she could hardly bring herself to speak civilly to Alf.

But Tom did not know these things and even if he had, it is doubtful whether they would have made much difference to him. He took on his responsibilities as head of the house bravely. It was his duty as the eldest son to run the farm and to provide for his mother and Molly. George would soon join him and he was glad of that, for the brothers had become close friends over the years. But Tom's white face and set expression spoke of his inner misery. Mary was deeply troubled about him, knowing how close he had been to his father. She feared lest his despair might even lead him to contemplate some terrible act of self-destruction or that his anger may spur him on to some yet more terrible act of vengeance. On several occasions she tried to speak to him, but even she could not penetrate the cloak of grief and rage that Tom had flung around himself.

There was someone else who was concerned about Tom. Kathy Hartley had been watching him. A sensitive young woman, she felt for him in his pain and loss. The death of her own mother when she needed her most had given her some understanding of what Tom must be feeling. She had wished for some opportunity to speak to Tom, but none had arisen until one afternoon late in 1755, some three months after Jack's death. Winter had set in and the sky was dull and threatening — it looked as if a blizzard was on its way. Tom had been out on the moors collecting his sheep in order to bring them down to their winter quarters. Kathy had been taking Mr Grimshaw a loaf of her newly-baked bread, as she had done several times before, knowing how often he neglected himself. Now, gathering up her long skirts, she was hurrying along the lane to reach her home before the storm broke. Just as she was passing Old Acre Farm she saw Tom coming down the hillside, skilfully guiding the last of his sheep.

Tom stopped as he saw Kathy. A rare smile greeted her, but soon the old haunted look of misery returned. 'Tom, you mustn't take on so, it's yerself you're hurting most' was all that the young woman managed to say.

'Yer don't understand, nobody does,' retorted Tom bitterly.

'I do, more than you ever think,' Kathy ventured. That was enough for Tom.

'Come into th' barn,' he said brusquely. 'I'll jest pen these sheep and join yer.' Kathy went into the barn and settled herself down on a bale of hay. Tom soon followed, finding another bale to sit on. Then Kathy listened as Tom poured out the whole sorry story: about Alice, whom Kathy well remembered as her own early playmate; about his mother's prayer on the night of the storm; about Farmer Greenwood's last words; about the way Patsy Walters had deceived him, about the all-consuming hatred he felt inside for Alf Sykes; but most of all about how he knew that he could not turn to God for help because it would mean that he must forgive Alf Sykes and that he would never do — never. It was a tangled, disjointed account, but once Tom had started there was no stopping him. Not since Farmer Greenwood's death, nine years ago now, had Tom been able to speak of his innermost feelings to anyone. Sensibly Kathy just let him talk, listening quietly without any interruptions.

Under the scaffold

'Wouldn't you feel like that if you were me?' he ended rather pathetically.

'Yes and no,' Kathy replied carefully. 'Yer know, Tom, when my Ma died, and I had to look after Annie, Dick and my Pa, I felt really angry inside. I was only thirteen and I needed Ma badly myself. I was angry against my circumstances but most of all angry against God for letting it happen — I was really blaming him for taking Ma away — and that's far worse than being angry against Alf Sykes.' Tom looked at the girl in surprise. She had always seemed so affectionate and even-tempered; he would never have guessed that she had known such inner turmoil. 'My Pa was so unhappy — he used to cry a lot, and that made it worse,' she went on. 'Sometimes I used to walk out on the moors by myself just to get away from it all. But when Mr Whitefield came back to Haworth not long after Ma died, I heard him say, "Till our hearts are broken and made contrite by the Spirit of our Lord Jesus Christ we shall always be charging God foolishly." And that's just what I was doing, Tom. I was charging God foolishly. I knew then that I didn't deserve anything from God except punishment for my sins.'

Tom was so surprised by all that Kathy had told him that for a few moments they sat in silence. At last Kathy said, 'I'd best go now or Pa will be wondering what's happened to me.' Picking the scraps of hay off her cloak, she stood up, but just before leaving she added in a low voice, 'Did yer hear that my Pa is goin' to get remarried?' No, Tom had not heard, and so Kathy went on, 'Widow Ogden from Stanhope is goin' to marry him. I canna understand what he sees in her, and do yer know, Tom, I don't think she likes me very much. I guess it's not goin' to be easy at home.'

At the door of the barn, Kathy suddenly turned. 'Why don't you come with me to St Michael's on Sunday,' she suggested.

Kathy

'We could meet at the back of the church and Mr Grimshaw would never see us.' How did she know that he would not wish the curate to see him? Kathy had read Tom's thoughts rightly. With no excuse left and a girl like Kathy inviting him, Tom agreed to go.

Heavy snow fell overnight and the winds from off the moors blew it into huge drifts, making the track from Old Acre Farm down to the village almost impassable. But Tom was used to such conditions and armed with a spade he dug a path for himself and his family to use. When Sunday came, Mary and Molly picked their way along Tom's path and managed to find seats inside the church. Tom waited until they had disappeared down the lane before he set out. It was a Communion Sunday and despite the wintry conditions hundreds of extra worshippers were expected to stream into the village for the services. Many would have to stand outside in the graveyard in the biting temperatures for, in spite of the recent enlargements to the church, the building was still unable to accommodate all who wished to be at the service. In view of this, Mr Grimshaw had announced that he would be preaching twice, first to those outside the building so that they would not stand around too long in the cold, and then again to those who had found a seat inside St Michael's.

Kathy was waiting for Tom around the side of the building in a place where Mr Grimshaw could not see them even though he had climbed onto a large tombstone, which gave him an excellent view of most who were gathered in the churchyard. It had been almost five years since Tom had attended a Sunday service and when Mr Grimshaw began his sermon the young man found it difficult at first to know quite what the curate was talking about. Then Tom caught the words 'prodigal son'; immediately his attention was arrested. It was a story he half-remembered, a parable Jesus had told about a son who had received numerous favours from his father, but he had cast them all aside, gone his own way and wasted all of his inheritance money.

In some ways Tom could see himself in that prodigal son, and even more so when the preacher pointed out that the son had ended up caring for pigs, as Tom now did. In desperate need the prodigal had decided to return to his father. But would his father forgive him and receive him back into the family? That was the question in Tom's mind. 'Yonder he comes, yonder he comes!' cried the preacher, pointing into the distance. 'Yonder he comes, all rag tag and bobtail.' Tom was so gripped by this time that almost before he could stop himself he had turned his eyes to the moors to see if he could catch a glimpse of the prodigal clothed in nothing but rags, coming home at last. Not only did the father in the parable forgive the son, but more than that he even gave him a welcome-home feast. And God too would welcome back those who were truly penitent, Mr Grimshaw assured his listeners.

Tom left the church that day a little brighter, a new glimmer of hope in his spirit. If that father had forgiven his son, perhaps God would forgive him too. But then he remembered Alf Sykes. He knew he could not expect forgiveness from God if he refused to forgive. And to forgive one who had wronged him so wickedly was something he felt he could never do — at least not until Alf Sykes had been paid back in some way for the evil he had done. Bitterness, anger and hatred were casting a chain around Tom's spirit and holding him prisoner.

The long cold winter months, the leaden grey skies and freezing conditions might well have added to the gloom that rested on Tom's spirit. Instead the days were brightened by his growing friendship with Kathy. The barn — that very barn that Tom and Jack had built together after the fire — became their secret meeting place, for as yet neither was prepared to let any one know that they were meeting. Kathy would steal across to Old Acre under cover of darkness, after work on the farm was over for the day. Here they would sit sheltered from the fierce winds that tore down from the moors above, and chat together. Kathy was a good listener, which was just as well because Tom was a good talker.

In spite of the busy days on the farm during the lambing season in the spring of 1756, followed by the sheep shearing, Tom found himself eagerly listening for the chime of the church clock as it marked the passing hours. He started the evening milking of the cows a little earlier, always hoping that Kathy would be able to finish her duties in time to come to the barn. Seldom was he disappointed. There in the semi-darkness of the barn, they enjoyed one another's company. There was always so much to say. Sometimes they discussed Mr Grimshaw's sermons, but mostly they just shared the happenings of a day, laughing together over trivial events and enjoying the fact that neither family knew of their secret friendship.

One night Tom told Kathy all about the day that he had discovered Jane Grimshaw up on the moors. Kathy had heard something of it from the local gossips but not from Tom himself. He went on to tell her of how sad he had felt when Jane had been taken off to school in Bristol and, most of all, of the way she had quoted a verse of a hymn just before she died. Tom remembered every word quite distinctly:

He has loved me, I cried,
he has suffered and died
to redeem such a rebel as me!

'Jane was not a rebel, Kathy,' Tom had said wistfully. 'She was gentle and kind. Alf Sykes sure needs redeeming, but I don't suppose he thinks so, and in any case, I'm not sure he's worth redeeming.'

Kathy thought for a moment and then said quietly, 'Yer know, Tom, I don't think any of us is worth redeeming; Alf Sykes never meant to kill your Pa. In a way I think he may already have suffered for what he has done. God can forgive and redeem even people who've done the most dreadful things.' Tom fell silent for a few moments and then changed the subject.

As they sat and chatted night after night in the barn, Tom had a growing attachment, mixed with a protective tenderness, for Kathy. But with it there was a respect and restraint that forbade him to take advantage of her friendship and trust. Never had he felt like this in his relationship with Patsy Walters. But one night as they sat side by side in the gloom of the barn Tom suddenly realized how much Kathy meant to him. 'Kathy, I do love you!' he blurted out suddenly. He threw his arm around her, drew her near and kissed her. Nor did Kathy push him away. How many minutes passed as they sat there together he could not say, but certainly neither he nor Kathy heard footsteps approaching the barn. Thirteen-year-old Molly had been getting curious as to why her older brother Tom disappeared almost every evening. She had half-guessed, but was not quite sure. Even Molly was taken by surprise, however, when she rushed into the barn to grab an armful of hay for Floss, the mare. With a crash she tripped over Kathy's legs, and landed on top of her brother. 'Oh! Eh! Miss Kathy! Tom! I'm real sorry,' she gasped as she picked herself up, bits of hay clinging to her hair and clothes. 'I niver knew you was here, really I did not.'

But the secret was out. Molly was as talkative as her brother Tom and before long all Molly's friends, and of course that meant their parents too, knew of the developing friendship between Tom

Kathy

Whittaker and Kathy Hartley. 'I guessed as much,' declared Big Bob's mother who was renowned for knowing everyone else's business. 'It's the best news I've heard for young Tom Whittaker for many a long day.'

15.
Prisoner of hope

The sense of excitement and anticipation in Haworth during the early days of August 1756 was strong: it was impossible to escape from it. George Whitefield was back in the area and had been preaching in many of the northern towns and villages. Birstall, Bradford, Tadcaster, had all received visits from the well-loved and sought-after preacher. Within a few days he was due in Haworth. But more than this — and certainly Tom pricked up his ears when he heard the news — two high-born ladies, members of the nobility, were travelling around with him. Selina, Countess of Huntingdon, was a person of whom many in Haworth had heard but few had met. She, and her sister-in-law Lady Margaret Ingham who lived only twenty-five miles away in Aberford, near Leeds, were accompanying Mr Whitefield on his travels.

Kathy urged Tom to come with her to hear the preacher. At least six thousand people were expected to crowd into the village; a number that would almost treble the entire population of Haworth together with that of the three adjacent villages that made up the parish. But Tom was not eager to attend. Memories of the first and only time he had heard the great preacher still remained clear in his mind although he had only been a boy of twelve at the time. He was torn between his affection for Kathy with his natural desire to please her, and his fear of the implications that the preaching might have for him. What if Mr Whitefield urged his hearers to forgive those who had wronged them, if they themselves wished to be forgiven for their sins? What if he should speak of the coming day when God would judge all men and women for the sins they had committed? Tom wished to hear about neither subject.

Tom's friendship with Kathy had grown close and strong. Together they roamed the moors hand in hand on warm summer evenings when work for the day was done. Together they listened to the songs of the skylarks from high above them or sat chatting by the streams of clear bubbling water that flowed down the hillside. Tom showed Kathy all the places that held memories for him. This was the hidden valley where he had found Jane after she had fallen and caught her foot; this was the very spot where he had lain down to sleep on that fateful night of the storm when Farmer Greenwood had found him. One place to which Tom did not take Kathy was Hoyle Syke Green where Mr Grimshaw had found the young people misbehaving themselves. He still felt a strong sense of shame as he thought of his conduct at that time.

During June 1756 Kathy's father, Robert Hartley, married Widow Ogden from Stanhope. Her first husband had died in the same smallpox epidemic that had carried away Kathy's own mother Jeanie. Having had no family of her own, Kathy's new stepmother had little understanding of young people. An irritable sort of woman, she was often impatient with Kathy and Dick and, as Kathy had anticipated, the situation in the home was frequently tense. Dick found it easier to ignore the newcomer but for Kathy the problem was most acute in terms of her relationship with her father. She had been his closest friend and confidante in the last six years and her stepmother soon proved herself to be both domineering and jealous.

Prisoner of hope

The fact that Kathy too had problems to face and sometimes felt resentment and anger simmering towards her stepmother was in a strange way an encouragement to Tom. If she had had no weaknesses, no need, he could well have felt a measure of despair in her company. Only one thing remained to prevent any further development of the affection between the two young people: Tom knew well that he could never venture any proposal of marriage to the girl he cared about so deeply until his own present uncertainty about spiritual things had been resolved. But how that could happen, he hardly knew. His attitudes and concerns had changed much since that snowy night six months earlier when he and Kathy had met unexpectedly and started their evening conversations in the barn. But Alf Sykes seemed always to be there standing between them — the very thought of him an ugly reminder to Tom of his own hatred and inability to forgive.

At last, however, Tom agreed that he would go with Kathy to hear George Whitefield preach. A heat wave that had already lasted for almost a week made 8 August, the day that the preacher was due in Haworth, the hottest day of the year. Apparently the scaffold pulpit was to be used for the first time. Mr Whitefield would climb out of the window of the church and stand on the wooden platform where he could be heard by the people inside the church and be seen as well as heard by those who were packed into the graveyard around it. Throughout the day crowds had been streaming into Haworth just as they had done on previous occasions — how news of the event had been carried to so many people, Tom could not imagine.

Tom and Kathy stood together near an outside wall of the graveyard. All around them men, women and young people were packed so tightly together that they scarcely had room to turn round. Tom was a little anxious lest Kathy should faint in the

Under the scaffold

heat, made much more intense by the crush of so many bodies. In the distance, not far from the foot of the scaffold, they could just see a tall, elegant-looking and well-dressed lady, her dark brown hair swept back from her strong features. Near her stood another lady, older, but attractive and with a gentle face. 'Those must be them two grand ladies as were comin',' Tom whispered to Kathy. Standing nearby, as if to protect his august visitors from the crush, was William Grimshaw himself.

At last a strange hush descended on that vast crowd. Every face was turned expectantly towards the scaffold pulpit. And at that very moment the preacher stepped out from the window and took his place beside the temporary lectern set up on the scaffold. On top of the lectern there appeared to be a cushion or perhaps it was a pillow, placed there to support an open Bible. Mr Whitefield looked much the same as Tom had remembered him from seven years earlier, only now it would seem that he had lost that youthful slim figure that Tom had recollected. For a few moments the preacher stood, his head bowed in silent prayer. Then raising both arms he called upon God to be present and to grant his blessing in the hearts of the people. That voice! It was just the same as Tom remembered it, and with a rush all the earlier memories flooded back.

'It is appointed unto men once to die, but after this the judgement',[1] cried the preacher in tones urgent, clear and arresting as he announced his text. Tom shuddered. That was just what he had most feared he might hear. At the very moment that Mr Whitefield was about to begin his message a loud scream suddenly broke from somewhere in the middle of the crowd — followed by a babble of voices. Whatever could have happened?

'I beg of you all to keep calm,' called the preacher as William Grimshaw pressed quickly through the crowd to see if he could discover the trouble. After a few moments' pause the crowd parted and Tom could see that someone was being carried through the passage that had been cleared. Then he saw the curate hurrying through the crowd once more to the foot of the scaffold.

'Brother Whitefield, Brother Whitefield!' he called out in his deep unmistakable voice, 'you stand amongst the dead and the dying — an immortal soul has been called into eternity. The destroying angel is passing over the congregation. Cry aloud and spare not! Cry aloud and spare not!' Tom began to tremble. This was worse than he could ever have imagined. Oh! Why had he agreed to come?

'*It is appointed unto men once to die, but after this the judgement*,' cried George Whitefield once more. Quite suddenly there was a second wild, terrifying shriek. This time it came from a spot very close to where the Countess of Huntingdon and Lady Margaret were standing. A second person had collapsed and died. Clearly the crush and intense heat had brought on a heart attack or similar condition. An awesome stillness — a stillness like death itself — rested over the congregation, so unnerving that Tom was plainly terrified. After a short time this second casualty was carried away. Then Mr Whitefield announced for the third time: '*It is appointed unto men once to die, but after this the judgement*.' Who would be next? The young were taken in death as well as the old, as Tom well knew, and he for one was acutely aware that he was not ready to face the judgement to come. Kathy stole her hand into his and gripped it tight. She too was frightened and they could never afterwards be quite sure whether she was steadying Tom or whether it was the other way round.

'Consider how dreadful your state will be at death, and after that the judgement,' cried the preacher. 'O be humbled, be humbled, I beseech you for your sins! Having spent so many years in sinning, what less can you do than be concerned to spend some hours in mourning for the same and be humbled before God?'[2] Tom scarcely heard a word of what Mr Whitefield was saying. That text, repeated three times over, drummed in his ears almost like the church bell tolling for a funeral. If Kathy had not been there he would have made a speedy escape as he had done before. And those unearthly shrieks haunted him day and night for weeks to come.

Kathy said all she could to help Tom but it seemed that her words passed unheeded. During the next few days Tom could scarcely eat or sleep. He went about his duties on the farm in a mechanical way, for his mind seemed elsewhere. Mary Whittaker sometimes went into Tom's attic room and sat with him at night when he could not sleep. And always it was those five words that rang ceaselessly in his mind: *but after this the judgement*. His neglect of God for ten or more years weighed heavily on his conscience; but even heavier was his inability to forgive. Now he felt himself in a prison — a prison of anger and hatred with bars so strong that he feared he could never escape.

At last, late one night, Tom's despair drove him to knock once again on that heavy studded door of Sowdens Farm where Mr Grimshaw lived. Everyone in the household was already in bed, but not William Grimshaw. It almost seemed as if the curate were waiting up for the young man. He had been watching Tom carefully but knew that he could not speak to him until Tom was ready. Ever since Tom had been a small child William Grimshaw had felt a special affection for the boy — he often prayed for him and particularly so since the death of Tom's father Jack.

Tom sat down miserably, his head buried in his hands. He did not begin to explain why he had come, and anyway Mr Grimshaw seemed to know already. 'Tom,' began the curate, 'no one can begin to be good until he knows that he is bad.' Tom nodded dumbly. It was his sins that had been haunting him day after day, and night after night as well. 'Nor can you begin to taste the sweetness of God's mercies until you have tasted the bitterness of your own misery,' he continued. Tom realized that Mr Grimshaw was speaking from his own experience for he recalled that when he had visited the family shortly after Alice had died, the curate

Entrance to Sowdens

had told them of his own desperate struggle to find forgiveness of sins.

Then the curate touched on the heart of Tom's problem: Alf Sykes. Tom was a prisoner to the anger and hatred he felt towards that bullying coward who had brought about his father's death. 'Tom,' continued Mr Grimshaw kindly, 'you are trying to find the power to forgive from within yourself. Not until you have found forgiveness for your own sins will you have the power to forgive the sins of others against you.' He quoted several verses from the Bible to the troubled young man, but one which Tom remembered was about Christ coming 'to proclaim liberty to the captives, and the opening of the prison to them that are bound'.³ Perhaps there would be hope for him after all before that terrible day of judgement.

'Only Christ can open the prison doors and set you free, Tom,' said Mr Grimshaw as Tom rose to go. 'And by the way, Mr Whitefield is coming back to Haworth in two weeks time. I much hope you will feel able to come.' Tom smiled wryly. Certainly if Kathy had her way he would be there. He left Sowdens in a brighter spirit than when he had come half an hour earlier, and creeping in by the back door of the farm, was soon sound asleep in his bed — more at peace than he had been for many weeks.

Autumn seemed to have come early that year, clothing the moors in purple. Shining cobwebs, lit up with the low rays of the October sun, hung from bush and tree. Many trees had already exchanged their greens for oranges and golds. As they wandered together across the moors, Kathy noticed that Tom seemed a little happier but she had the wisdom not to question him too much. She had, however, managed to persuade him to accompany her to hear Mr Whitefield once more when he returned to Haworth on 10 October. As it was a Communion Sunday, thousands were expected to throng into Haworth again, even though Charles Wesley himself was also in the north of England and preaching at Birstall, near Leeds, that same Sunday. Before long Tom saw the scaffold pulpit being erected outside the window of the church once more. He looked at it with a mixture of anticipation and dread.

And still they came, streaming up Main Street or along West Lane as had happened in the past. Some people were prepared to wait for hours in order to find a place to stand where they could both see and hear the preacher. Even though his brother George was now helping him on the farm, Tom was not free until late afternoon. Tom's mother and his sister Molly had both secured seats within the church itself. But by the time Tom and Kathy arrived, there seemed scarcely a corner left into which they could squeeze. What were they to do? Then Tom spotted a space where they could stand, in fact the only space available, right under the scaffold itself. True they could not see the preacher, but certainly they would have no difficulty in hearing.

Tom found his heart thumping as he waited for the preacher to begin. The sound of footsteps right above their heads and the sudden hush that descended upon that huge congregation told Tom and Kathy that the preacher had stepped out of the window and the service was about to start. *'Turn to the stronghold, you prisoners of hope, even today do I declare that I will render double unto you,'*[4] announced that clear moving voice as Whitefield gave out his text. Tom jumped in surprise at the words. A prisoner, yes, that was just what Mr Grimshaw had called him.

Haworth Church as it was in 1756.[5]

Under the scaffold

Tom knew that he was a prisoner, but a 'prisoner of hope'? That was another matter. From the preacher's first word, the young man stood riveted. Never had he felt like this in his life before. Jesus Christ, explained Mr Whitefield, was a stronghold; he was a place of refuge to which the prisoners, held captive by their sinning and their circumstances, could escape in their need and despair. Instead of being chained by guilt and sin they could become willing bond-slaves of Jesus Christ — his prisoners of hope. And Christ would give to his prisoners of hope 'double' — double joy even now, double power to forgive, freedom from that terrible day of judgement and the hope of heaven to come. Tears flowed freely and unashamedly down Tom's cheeks and Kathy wept with him. It seemed to Tom that Mr Whitefield had a private knowledge of every thought, every sin, every action and every longing that he had experienced since those days just after Alice had died.

'O that I might persuade one poor soul to fly to Jesus Christ! Make him your refuge, your stronghold, you prisoners of hope,' urged the preacher as he closed his message. 'Then, however cast down you may have been, you may hope in God and yet praise him for his deliverance from the prison house of your sins. God help those who have believed to hope more and more in his salvation, till faith be turned into vision, and hope into fruition. Even so, Lord Jesus. Amen and Amen.'

As that last 'Amen' died away, Tom turned to Kathy, joy shining through his tears. At last, at long last, Tom had found a refuge for his soul, a stronghold against all the troubles of life. Under the scaffold, hidden even from the eyes of the preacher, a young man had discovered that Christ could give him deliverance from the power of his sins and would give him the strength to forgive. Christ had indeed opened the prison door and released one who had long been bound. At last Tom Whittaker knew for himself what William Grimshaw had told him long ago that only by faith in the power and work of Christ can a poor sinner be justified in God's sight.

Haworth Church after further rebuilding work

16.
Forgiven

William Grimshaw's genial face was wreathed with smiles when Tom knocked at the door of Sowdens the following day. Tom did not even need to explain why he had come or what had happened to him under the scaffold. The evident joy and relief from the dark oppression under which he had struggled for so long was written all over the young man's face and told its own story. Mr Grimshaw was one of the most humble and least self-centred men that Tom had ever met. Whether it was his own preaching or that of Mr Whitefield, Mr Wesley or anyone else mattered little to him. God had answered his prayers for his young neighbour after these many years.

Late that same night after Tom had done his last-minute check around the farmyard, he discovered that his mother had not yet gone to bed, but was sitting by the kitchen fire on her own. Pulling up the kitchen chair Tom sat down beside her. He normally had no difficulty in expressing himself, but now it was not easy. Yet he wanted to share with Mary that experience of gladness and release that he had so recently found as he realized at last that Christ could set him free from the prison house of those dark and angry thoughts that had almost destroyed him. He had been forgiven for his many sins and for the long years of neglect and indifference to God. Now he had only one desire burning in his heart: to live to please God while he could. He told his mother about Jack's final words to him: that Jack had hoped his son might one day serve God in place of him. Who could tell? Perhaps he might yet be able to fulfil his father's last wish. Mary went to bed that night too happy to sleep — with a joy that could only be expressed in tears as she saw an answer to her long and earnest prayers for Tom.

Nothing now stood between Tom and Kathy. He knew she loved him. He had read it in her eyes, in her understanding and patience, in her many small acts of kindness — and yet somehow he felt unable to ask her to marry him. Perhaps it was a sense of unworthiness that held him back. His respect for her was so deep that he feared lest he should be a disappointment to her, lest he should prove unable to live up to her expectations. But late one December night, more than two months after Tom and Kathy had stood together under the scaffold listening to George Whitefield's sermon, Tom's diffidence and fears were swept away under the power of a stronger emotion.

Fresh snow had been falling, covering the bare winter trees with a fairy-like beauty. Tom was checking that the animals were secure, with enough fresh hay, before bolting the doors for the night. Then he heard the sound of a familiar footstep. Looking up sharply he saw Kathy approaching, her cloak thrown roughly around her shoulders, her head bowed, her dark hair covered in snow.

'Kathy! Whatever can yer be doing out at this time o'night?' he cried. Then he saw that her face was swollen with crying. 'What's the matter?' he gasped. Throwing herself into Tom's arms, Kathy sobbed inconsolably. Tom led the distressed girl into the kitchen and sat down with her beside the dying fire, one arm around her shoulder. He waited until she was calm enough to explain her trouble. At last through her tears Kathy was able to tell Tom that her stepmother had become increasingly jealous of her, and had grown ever more bitter because of the love that she had for her father, and her father for her. Earlier that night things had reached crisis point. Unable to contain her resentment any longer, Kathy's stepmother had actually told the girl that she was no longer wanted or needed in the home; she must leave just as soon as she could make alternative arrangements and how glad she would be to see her go. Nor had Kathy's father been strong enough to resist his second wife's aggressive demands.

'That's dreadful, Kathy. I'll, I'll, I'll...' Tom expostulated angrily. But he never said just what he would do. Strange to relate, he was almost glad — a strong sense of exhilaration had gripped him. At last he could see that Kathy really needed him: that she was frightened and vulnerable and longed for his protection and love. '*This* is going to be your home now, Kathy,' he declared. 'You're mine, mine, and this is where you're loved and wanted! Never, never, never will anyone ever turn yer away again.' He had almost surprised himself by the strength of his feelings. And before many moments had passed the two were locked into an embrace that put all Kathy's doubts about Tom's love away for ever.

When they looked up they saw Mary standing in the doorway with a mixture of surprise and joy written on her face. 'Ma, could yer make Kathy and me some soup and then I'll be atakin' her back home,' Tom asked in an embarrassed voice, 'and Ma! She's mine now!' he added triumphantly. It was Mary's turn to cry: but they were tears of happiness for Tom and Kathy.

Tom lost no time in making arrangements for the marriage ceremony to take place. Not for Tom and Kathy any grand occasion, with bridesmaids and flowers, and a flowing white dress. Nor could Tom even afford to buy a ring to mark their union, but dressed in the best clothes they possessed the young couple took their vows. And the joy that glowed in their hearts as Mr Grimshaw solemnly declared them to be man and wife was none the less real for all that. There would be no such thing as a honeymoon, nor even a day off work, but in the evening after the ceremony Tom harnessed Floss to the cart and set off down the lane to Meadow Field Farm to fetch all Kathy's possessions and bring them across to Old Acre. Robert Hartley was standing at the door to wave his daughter off, a strange mixture of joy and sorrow on his face. Kathy's stepmother was nowhere to be seen. Before Tom cracked his whip to drive away he told his kindly neighbour that if ever he wished to call in to see his daughter he would be more than happy to welcome him at Old Acre.

Mary too was glad to receive Kathy into the home. George and Tom were both hungry young men and at fifty-four Mary was well aware that the cooking, spinning and tasks on the farm were becoming more than her strength would allow. Fifteen-year-old Molly was beginning to think of her own future. She could go into service like her sister Margaret had done, but the girl was much more attracted to the possibility of some young man asking for her hand in marriage. Vivacious and sociable, Molly had always been popular in the village, and if she should marry, her mother had scarcely known how she would manage without her. But now, with Kathy's coming, she had no more to worry about.

One snowy night soon after Tom and Kathy's marriage, they were surprised to hear a knock on the farm door. Who should be standing there but Mr Grimshaw?

'Tom,' he began, 'I've promised to preach in Bingley tonight, and I fear the track across the moors may well be covered over with new snow. Would yer like to come wi' me? You know the moors that well, and together we will not lose our way.' Bingley lay five miles away across the moors and Tom was well aware that if the curate had promised to go he would most certainly fulfil his promise. For an answer, Tom was already taking down his lantern and putting on his heavy boots. Together the two men set off, the snow whirling in their faces. Arriving at last they found a small barn lined with wooden benches already filled to capacity, despite the freezing temperatures and the storm.

Quickly unbuttoning his coat William Grimshaw stepped up to the makeshift lectern and gave out the words of a hymn. It was his favourite hymn:

Come we that love the Lord
and let our joys be known;
join in the song with sweet accord,
and thus surround the throne.

'The people sang like thunder,' wrote another young man who was present on that same occasion as he recalled it later in life. Tom joined in the singing but was quite unable to hear his own voice above the sound of the rest. He had never experienced anything like it. Because of the intensity of the cold he could see his breath as he sang, but he hardly seemed aware of the bitter elements. The text the curate announced was, '*Glory to God in the highest, and on earth peace, goodwill toward men*'. Glancing round Tom saw the looks of serious concern written on many faces as Mr Grimshaw spoke of the frightening state of men and women who would perish unless they knew the way of peace with God. As the preacher continued Tom could see the relief and joy evident all around as they heard of the hope of forgiveness through the mercy of Christ.

When they made their way homeward that night, Tom realized that to have accompanied Mr Grimshaw on that trek across the moors was in itself a service to God. 'If ever yer would like me to come wi' you again,' he ventured, 'I'd be that glad as long as Kathy don't mind.' And that was how Tom began to accompany William Grimshaw on some of his preaching excursions. He soon learnt that the curate of Haworth had two major preaching rounds which he tried to cover in alternate weeks, sometimes preaching up to thirty times in any one week. Little wonder then that John Wesley, who still visited Haworth regularly, said of his friend: 'A few such as him would make a nation tremble. He carries fire wherever he goes.'

As winter turned at last to spring, Tom and George worked far into the night coping with the lambing season. 'We could do with some extra help on the farm,' Tom told Grimshaw one day when he reluctantly felt he would not be able to accompany him to Otley, some fifteen miles away. 'If yer know of anyone who might be suitable, could yer let me know?'

One Saturday, early that summer, Grimshaw was back at Old Acre Farm. 'Would you like to come wi' me to Colne, Tom?' he asked. 'I'd be glad of the company if George and Kathy could spare you.' Tom hesitated. It was the first time he had done so, and the curate did not need to ask why. 'We'll go a back way, Tom,' he reassured his young friend. He knew well that Tom would not wish to pass the spot where Jack had fallen and injured himself.

Tom had another unspoken fear. What if he should catch a glimpse of Alf Sykes? How would he react? Yes, he had forgiven him, and no longer bore any animosity towards him. But to see him again? Tom was not sure how he would feel. However, he did not like to admit that this caused him any problems, and so agreed to accompany Mr Grimshaw. Saddling Floss, he was soon ready to set off, and Kathy had provided some of her home-made bread for her husband and curate to take with them on their way.

Forgiven

When they arrived at Colne and had tied up their horses, Tom was surprised at the numbers already gathered to hear Mr Grimshaw preach. Without delay the curate climbed up on to the mounting block outside the local tavern and announced his text: *'There is joy in the presence of the angels of God over one sinner who repents'*. A strange silence fell on that large crowd, many of whom had come into town for market day and had stayed on to hear the preaching prior to hurrying home before nightfall. 'If the angels rejoice over one sinner who repents, what must be the joy in the heart of the Son of God when you turn from your sins! Think of the sorrows and sufferings he endured to bring one sinner back to God. Can Christ love your soul and you are prepared to throw it away and your eternal happiness with it? O my hearers, repent! repent! before it is too late. God still waits to be gracious to you. Christ still stands offering his blood and merits freely to you. Your conscience is accusing you. And yes, the devil is waiting for your death that he may have you into hell unless you repent...'

Just as Mr Grimshaw was coming to the end of his sermon, Tom saw something that made the colour drain from his cheeks. There at the back of the crowd was Alf Sykes. Tom tried to shuffle round to a place where his old antagonist could not see him. But as he did so, he noticed an amazing thing. The tears were running down poor Alf Sykes' twisted unhappy face. Mr Grimshaw had noticed it too.

'Yes, for you too, poor sinner,' he pleaded, directing his words as if to Alf alone. 'It does not matter what you have done. How far you have sunk, how wicked you have been. Christ waits to show mercy and forgiveness. Even if everyone else casts you out, Christ will receive you and there is joy in his heart over one sinner — yes, even one like you — when you repent.'

Under the scaffold

Tom could bear it no longer. As Mr Grimshaw's last words died away he was making his way around the outside of the crowd to where Alf was standing. Alf saw him coming and buried his face in his hands. 'Tom, I'm right sorry for what I did,' he managed to say at last through his tears. 'Can yer ever forgive me?'

'I've bin as bad as you in another way, Alf,' Tom replied steadily. 'Yer never meant to kill my Pa — and Alf, I'm real sorry that I hated you like I did. Christ has forgiven me, and I want yer to know that I forgive yer too.' Alf was now sobbing like a child, and as the crowd slowly dispersed Tom sat down with him. Gradually the whole sorry story came out. Alf had not been able to hold down a steady job since that day. He had desperately wanted to apologize to Tom, but he knew well enough that Tom would not accept anything that he said. A social outcast, he had given up all hope. Twice he had sunk to such depths of misery that he had attempted to take his life.

At that moment Mr Grimshaw approached the two young men, and while he talked with Alf on his own, Tom went off to fetch the horses. When he returned, leading Floss and Mr Grimshaw's white pony, Alf was smiling. His usually ugly face even looked attractive in a strange sort of way. And Tom had one more thing to say to Alf. 'When I've had a word wi' my brother, George, and wi' my Ma and Kathy, I think we could fix yer up with a job at the farm. I reckon it would be good for yer to get out of Colne anyway.'

With those words Tom had won the hardest battle of his life: the battle to forgive someone who had wronged him as grievously as Alf Sykes had done. God had forgiven him his sins for the sake of Jesus Christ and he had given Tom a strength he could never have imagined before to forgive Alf Sykes.

Forgiven

Alf did come to work on the farm, and a faithful and diligent worker he proved. It gave Tom the opportunity to spend more time accompanying Mr Grimshaw on his travels and gradually a desire was born in Tom's heart that perhaps he too might one day become a preacher — and hold forth God's message of forgiveness to men and women crushed by a sense of their sins and need. But that is another story.

Notes

Chapter 1

1. If you perish, you will perish with the sound of the gospel in your ears.
2. The average age of the population of Haworth at the time was 26 years. 46% of the children died before they reached the age of 7.

Chapter 2

1. The Works of John Owen, *The Doctrine of Justification by Faith,* vol. 5.

Chapter 5

1. 'Old moss-crop' was a term of endearment Grimshaw sometimes used when he addressed the elderly members of his congregation.

Chapter 8

1. Or 'setts' as they are more correctly called.
2. Isaiah 35:4.

Chapter 10

1. Quotations from Whitefield's *Sermons on Important Subjects,* London, 1867, p.525.

Chapter 15

1. Hebrews 9:27.
2. George Whitefield, *Sermons on Important Subjects,* 1867, p.370.
3. Isaiah 61:1.
4. Zechariah 9:12.
5. The scaffold pulpit was placed between the 3rd and 4th windows.

Other titles by the author

The nine-day Queen of England — Lady Jane Grey
254 pages, ISBN 0 85234 579 8

Lives turned upside down
160 pages, ISBN 0 85234 521 6

Our hymn-writers and their hymns
400 pages, ISBN 0 85234 585 2

Seeing the invisible
160 pages, ISBN 0 85234 407 4

all published by Evangelical Press

For further reading

William Grimshaw of Haworth
368 pages, ISBN 0 85151 732 3 (hardback)
　　　　　　ISBN 0 85151 734 X (paperback)

published by Banner of Truth

A wide range of excellent books on spiritual subjects is available from Evangelical Press. Please write to us for your free catalogue or contact us by e-mail.

Evangelical Press
Faverdale North, Darlington, Co. Durham, DL3 0PH, England

e-mail: sales@evangelicalpress.org

Evangelical Press USA
P. O. Box 825, Webster, New York 14580, USA

e-mail: usa.sales@evangelicalpress.org

web: http://www.evangelicalpress.org